To Neil,

Your friendship has been of the sweetest in my life - Thank You for

BEYOND MY WILDEST DREAMS

being!

Love always

Kimmie

Lift Off

Beyond My Wildest Dreams
diary of a **UFO** abductee

a true story by
Kim Carlsberg

illustrated by
Darryl Anka

BEAR & COMPANY
PUBLISHING
SANTA FE, NEW MEXICO

LIBRARY OF CONGRESS CATALOGING-IN-PUBLICATION DATA

Carlsberg, Kim, 1955–

   Beyond my wildest dreams : diary of a UFO abductee / a true
story by Kim Carlsberg ; illustrated by Darryl Anka.

      p.   cm.

   ISBN 1-879181-25-8

   1. Unidentified flying objects—Sightings and encounters.
2. Carlsberg, Kim 1955–   —Diaries. 3. Abduction. I. Title.

TL789.3.C367 1994

001.9'42'092—dc20   95-5181

[B]   CIP

Bear & Company, Inc.
Santa Fe, NM 87504-2860

Art Direction by Kim Carlsberg

Illustrations © 1995 by Darryl Anka except for pages 2, 5, 23, 67, 71, 85, 151,
      199, 221, 265 © 1995 by Kim Carlsberg

Calligraphy by Kathleen Chambers

Graphic Design by Sandy Gentry & Johnny Lynch

Author Photo by Sharyl Noday

Cover Design by Lightbourne Images

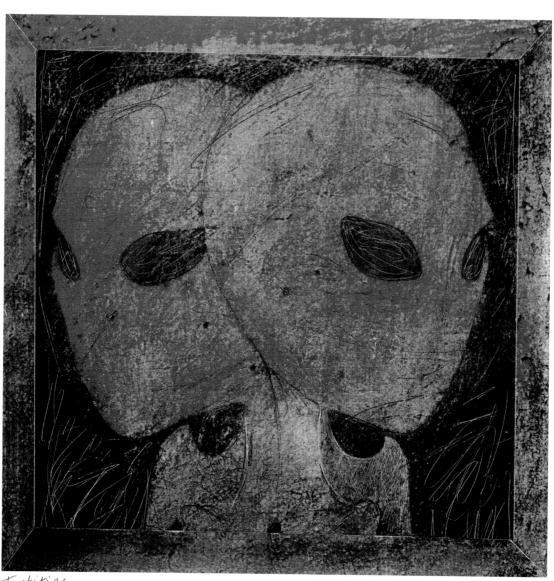

Entities

DEDICATION

It is my hope to bring about a broader awareness of close encounters and their reason for being in order to pave a smoother road for the next generation of chosen children on both sides of the veil.

This book is dedicated to all of these children, but in particular April, Aqua, Opal, and those I cannot name. The price they paid for life will be understood by only a few, but it echoes throughout eternity. May God bless and keep them! 👽

ACKNOWLEDGMENTS

I want to thank The Mutual UFO Network (MUFON), The Center For UFO Studies (CUFOS), and Close Encounter Research Organization (CERO) for their understanding and support through the profoundly difficult periods when no one else was there. I would also like to thank and salute all the abductees, researchers, authors, and members of the media who have—and continue to—put forth the truth in the face of ridicule and ignorance. You have provided an opportunity for me and many others to rebuild lives left shattered in the wake of contact. ☻

AUTHOR'S NOTE

This is not a research book. This is a sociological, cultural, and artistic response to my personal experiences with the UFO/abduction phenomenon.

As an artist and photographer, I feel it is appropriate to present my experiences in the form that is most natural to me. Therefore, rather than a simple chronicle of events, this book is an art piece and was created in that spirit. 👽

Moon

THE ART

The illustrations in this book were carefully designed to be accurate reflections of my experiences, as well as a visual representation of a larger outlook.

It is my personal belief that the phenomenon known as "abduction" spans not only all continents and cultures, but quite possibly the entire history of humankind.

It is for this reason I wanted to blend a wide variety of historical and cultural styles with an array of artistic techniques to further emphasize that idea in an original and provocative visual manner.

The fulfillment of this desire was made possible through the talent and dedication of one brilliant artist, who is an extremely evolved soul and a cherished friend—Darryl Anka. Thank you, Darryl!

The illustrations, while being as representative as possible of the actual events, include some additional artistic elements that are symbolic.

It was impossible to relate all of my experiences in this book, but I did want to present all the different types of spacecraft I have encountered. They are included as thumbnail sketches throughout the book wherever space was available.

Many abductees have described various alien symbols glimpsed in their encounters. In one experience, I was shown a wall of glyphs, but as often happens, when I return from

experiences, the details of the encounters are difficult to remember.

The one symbol I do recall was worn as an emblem on the chest of an alien's form-fitting body suit. It resembled our letter "A," though I doubt it has any connection to our language. We have included this symbol in several pieces of the art throughout the book. ☮

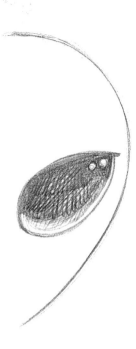

Beyond My Wildest Dreams

CONTENTS

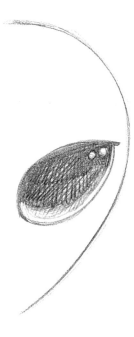

Beyond My Wildest Dreams

COLOR PLATES

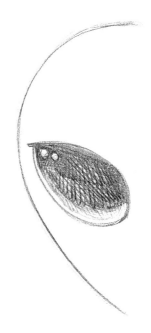

Beyond My Wildest Dreams

WHAT "DREAMS" ARE MADE OF

A critical point I want to make to the reader is that I have chosen the term "dreams," shown in quotes, to describe some of my alien encounters, even though I am fully aware of the solid reality of my experiences. *It should be understood the term "dream" is not meant to be taken literally.*

The nature of abduction, the intentions of the aliens, and the psychological makeup and belief systems of individuals all determine where "contact" falls within the human psyche —such as real experiences, hallucinations, and dreams.

In my particular case, as in most cases, the aliens control the abductee's consciousness to suppress the memories of the encounters. They use drugs, post-hypnotic suggestions, and a variety of other mind-altering techniques. There is also the natural protection of our own mind to dismiss that which it cannot contextualize appropriately.

Many frightening close encounters are cloaked and stored in what psychologists term *screen memories*. The mind, when confronted with an event too threatening, and beyond comprehension, will literally disguise the occurrence with a false memory that is more acceptable and less intimidating to the personality. Common screen memories of Grey aliens are owls, cats, deer, or other animals with large or slanted eyes.

I thoroughly realize how far-reaching the next statement sounds and I risk "putting off" readers before they get started,

but I believe it is essential to understanding our relationship with the alien visitors.

It is my personal conclusion they are not only extraterrestrial, but they are extradimensional in origin. This does not mean they are not real. It means they emerge into our "density" and "solidify." Many times the abductee is physically taken back to the alien "reality." Their realm is not natural to the structure of the human psyche or ego; therefore, the ego's ability to comprehend the experience is minimized. If these events are remembered at all, they usually maintain a dreamlike quality. *Again, this is why I am using the term "dream" to describe actual extraterrestrial encounters.*

Unlike other abductees I've met, most of whom have only vague, fragmented memories, I am fully conscious through many of the abductions. A couple of hunches come to mind as to why I am not always susceptible to the aliens' methods and why my own perception is often less impaired.

There are a few things about my personal biology which may interfere with the aliens' attempts at physical manipulation. I am extremely healthy and health conscious, but my reaction to any kind of drug is extreme. I am deadly allergic to all antibiotics, yet on the opposite end of the spectrum it sometimes takes up to ten shots of novocaine before a dentist can get a numbing effect for a simple filling. I've actually been sent home without dental work because the dentist gave up. So maybe the aliens' drugs don't work well on my particular body.

The other hunch is that my mental homework paid off. My life's passion has been the study of consciousness. I have a library filled with books on the power of the mind and have engaged in meditation as a regular practice for twenty years. Therefore, my psyche may be a little more resistant to outside suggestions and more capable of perceiving accurately in "unfamiliar surroundings."

But there are just as many times when I find myself in an in-between state, not knowing in these moments what is real and what is an illusion. Because of this fact, and because almost all of my contacts occur in the darkest hours before dawn, the term "dream" best describes events I felt were bordering on another reality. My consciousness has gradually adapted to the aliens' realm, so the dreamlike quality is dissipating and I am now fully alert most of the time during my encounters. Experiences in which I was clearly conscious at the time are labeled as conscious abductions.

In 1992, I did a series of four hypnotic regressions to aid in breaking through some of the more belligerent blocks in my memory. I was ready to confront certain abductions I knew occurred, but contained specific details too devastating for my conscious mind to recall. The sessions were successful in retrieving the buried memories, although I did not recall dates. Some of that information is important to the whole picture, so I have placed excerpts where they fit logically into the chronology of the book. ☻

Dreams

A FISH STORY

Throughout our lives we were led to believe in many things. We were led to believe in peace, family, and brotherly love, yet we live in a world filled with war, broken families, and violent crime. What we were led to believe in were ideals, but what we live in is reality.

We were led to believe if we were ever contacted by an alien race, it would resemble a scene from *Close Encounters of the Third Kind.* Another ideal! The reality is, contact is happening here and now, and it just doesn't fit the ideal.

We were led to believe in "government for the people, by the people," although our leaders have blatantly lied for over forty years about the mass of UFO evidence they keep "Above Top Secret."

We were led to believe communication with aliens would be as simple as programming a computer to repeat their sounds. The reality is, they don't use sound to communicate. They not only speak mind to mind, they speak to a portion of our consciousness that we are hardly aware exists.

We were sure it would be as simple as a humanoid form from another planet landing on solid ground. The truth is they are not only physically, mentally, and emotionally different, they are not limited to the laws of our physical reality.

They are to us as we are to the creatures of the sea. We show up in the oceans although we do not live there naturally.

Fish Story

We study, impact, and even kill. Our intentions are not hostile, they are merely curiosity and survival.

To the creatures of the sea we are elusive. We do not show up to the leaders of the fish community to announce our presence and intention. We drop in from an atmosphere which to them may not even exist. We take what we need and leave.

Most fish will probably reject the tale of the unfortunate fish who speaks of being ripped from his home by some large, curved metallic object. They will scoff when he complains he was squeezed until he bled, went unconscious, and woke up back in the water. To the fish it may be the most traumatic moment of his existence, even though he was one of the lucky ones: he was thrown back. To the fisherman it was a moment forgotten five minutes later.

The sooner the fish community gets wise to the fishermen, the better off they will be. I'm not saying the fishermen are bad, they are just fishermen. I'm not saying the aliens are bad, they are just aliens.

The fishermen aren't interested in learning the languages of the ocean's occupants. If the fish want to complain to the fisherman, they must learn his language and seek him out. Not an easy task for the fish, but if they accomplish it, they are going to be a highly evolved species. ♥

INTRODUCTION

One ordinary night, in the middle of an ordinary life, I had an extraordinary "dream." I fell through "the Looking Glass" into another world. However, unlike the children's fable, the place was real, and even more bizarre than the realm visited by Alice.

It has been six years since my first visit to that alien place, and since then I have come to understand many things about it and its inhabitants. But with each new understanding, more questions are raised than answered. Modern philosopher Werner Erhard recently proposed that instead of constantly seeking answers, we must learn to live in the question of what it means to be human. Whitley Streiber, a fellow abductee, prescribed in his book, *Transformation,* that we must learn to live at a high level of uncertainty. They have both described the new neighborhood in which the aliens have compelled my mind to dwell.

I have traced the edge of another reality. I am but a mere child on that foreign shore; tugged by the current of curiosity, while dreading the cold of an uncharted abyss. 👽

"It's not what happens to you,
it's what you do with what happens!"

– Bashar

RUDE AWAKENING
Conscious Abduction
Summer 1988

Dear Diary:

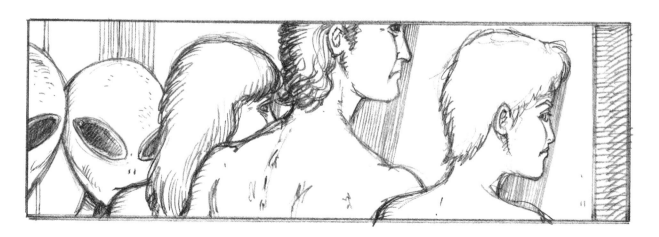

think I'm losing my mind. I hope so, because if what happened to me last night was real, I don't know how I'll be able to live with it. But I want to remember every last detail!

I arrived home late after a ten-hour shoot, completely exhausted. It was after midnight and Greg was already snoring, so I quietly slipped into bed beside him. I fell asleep quickly but abruptly woke to find I was no longer in our bed. I was standing in what seemed to be an elevator.

Instantly, I felt claustrophobic, not due to the small enclosure, but due to the fact I was packed in with many other bodies and jammed into a blind corner. Although I felt I was entrapped by sentient beings, the stench of rotting organic matter was suffocating. I didn't know where I was, how I got there, or how I could have been taken from my bed in the middle of the night without waking up, but there I stood with my nose pressed against the steel door.

I felt paralyzed, but my mind was alert. I couldn't even move my head from side to side, so out of the corner of my left eye I strained to see the person next to me. A familiar face, pained with confusion, was strangely unaware of my presence. It was my old boyfriend, David. There was another woman standing next to him. I couldn't see her physically but something told me she was there. I also had the idea she was a makeup artist. I don't know where these thoughts came from, and I didn't have time to think about it before the door opened and I was pushed into a large room. What I saw next was horrifying!

The room I had just been shoved into looked like a huge hospital ward. I couldn't believe my eyes! All through the stark room were rows of operating tables that were only a couple of feet off the ground. They were occupied by unconscious human beings—at least I hoped they were just unconscious. I couldn't focus on the humans long enough to determine if they were breathing; my eyes went straight to the creatures who were working on them.

They were little naked things with oversized bald heads, big

Rude Awakening I

black eyes, and bodies like cheap dolls void of detail, down to the absence of genitalia. The skin was off-white and I thought they looked like anorexic Pillsbury dough boys.

I stared at the table closest to me. The man lying on it was a Caucasian male in his forties. He was completely out. Two of the creatures were working on his limp body; one cradled his head while the other examined his wrist. I became more convinced the humans were dead instead of unconscious and I thought I was going to be next, prompting me to scream hysterically!

To my right stood four beings who seemed to be in charge. Two were identical to the "dough boys," only taller, about five feet rather than three-and-a-half feet. The other two were distinctly different. I squinted my eyes, thinking my vision was blurred, but realized something else was wrong. The figures of the other two beings seemed to be phasing in and out of the room as if only partly materialized. Their bodies were nondescript forms about nine feet tall and looked like waterfalls of energy.

In reaction to my outburst, one of the two taller bald creatures rushed up and slapped me on the back of the neck. I felt myself passing out like I had just been anesthetized. The other tall one stepped in front of me and just stared with huge, black, dead eyes, waiting for my collapse. I thought that hideous face was the last thing I would ever see!

I woke up later in a smaller room and immediately became hysterical again. I was on a cold metal table with one of those nasty creatures skulking in the darkness beside me. I sensed its

task had been completed and it was awaiting further instruction from some invisible authority. The room was unlit and the temperature was freezing. I don't know what happened to me in that ghastly metallic cave, but I know I've only felt that out of control one other time in my life—on that sickening evening when I was raped. I didn't know what these creatures were, what they wanted, or why they chose me, but they drugged me, kidnapped me from my bed and, now that they seemed to be finished, I expected the worst.

I could see another, larger room through the open arched doorway. This room was well lit, so when a figure appeared in the door, the being was silhouetted. My first thought was: this creature must be dying from cancer. Its back-lit hair was patchy, like that of someone undergoing radiation treatment. I realized it was female and I cried out to her for mercy, "Can't you see how terrified I am, won't you please help me?" Her apathetic response shocked me out of my hysteria. "Why don't you stop being such a big baby, this will be over with soon enough." At that moment, it was obvious to me these things had no emotion. And what did she mean by "over with?" I was so stunned by her words I couldn't respond. Then I realized she had not spoken at all; I was hearing her thoughts. She was using telepathy and I understood her perfectly.

The next thing I knew I was back in my bed lying next to Greg. He hadn't moved from the position he was in when I first went to sleep. How could he have slept through what had just

happened to me?* I was heartbroken, angry, and confused. It must have been late because I only lay there a short while before Greg got up for his routine 5:30 A.M. workout, at which time I pretended to be asleep. There was no way I could have explained why I was awake so early and I didn't want to have to try.

When I was sure Greg was gone, I pulled myself out of bed and walked over to the window. Seeing the lifeguard tower on the beach snapped my mind back to the other strange event that had occurred a few weeks prior. Both episodes were too bizarre to be mere coincidence; they must be related, and the implications were staggering. An unbelievable loneliness crept into my blood like I had just witnessed the death of my world and all that I loved. ♥

*Several years later in my research, I learned the reason Greg did not stir from his sleep state was due to the aliens' ability to "switch off" the people not involved in the abduction. They render the other persons unconscious and paralyzed. Greg couldn't have helped me even if he wanted to. I also realized the "thoughts" about the makeup artist were my first experiences at receiving telepathic information. Telepathy is the aliens' natural form of communication and, for some unknown reason when I am in their presence, I automatically assume the same telepathic ability myself.

Rude Awakening II

A FEW WEEKS EARLIER…

having served my time I had recently been released from the renowned Los Angeles Art Center "Prison" of Design (as my classmates and I fondly called it), where I majored in photography. Out in the working world only a short while, I still suffered from visions of grandeur, but the Hollywood film-production totem pole quickly burst my bubble.

I accepted a job as assistant photographer to help shoot a magazine cover and spread for Pee Wee Herman's feature film, *Big Top Pee Wee*.

Life magazine flew in a "name" photographer from New York, and I broke my back for days hauling and setting up camera equipment at the whim of my boss. The real eye opener came at the end of the shoot as I watched my boss step into her stretch limo, while I and the rest of the crew stood by sweat-soaked and sore, having done all the work and been paid beans.

I decided then and there I had to do better than assisting. Even though I lacked the confidence that comes with years of experience, the Art Center had gifted me with the same technical knowledge as my boss. What it didn't gift me with was a limo, but at that moment I was happy to have my trusty Camero to take me home.

At 1:30 A.M. I was able to cruise the Santa Monica Freeway at 55 MPH. Driving the speed limit was a nice change from the normal clutch of L.A. traffic. My car raced through the concrete

canyon created by overpasses, malls, and containment walls, and I entered the curving, graffiti-lined tunnel that poured me onto the Pacific Coast Highway. The tunnel was my decompression chamber, transitioning me from the dense, synthetic cityscape into the organic expanse of the Pacific Ocean.

The home stretch ended where Sunset Boulevard meets the sea. I turned off the coast highway and onto the winding road that dead-ends behind the home my boyfriend and I lovingly called "the Pink Castle." The Spanish-style dwelling commands a sweeping view of the entire Santa Monica Bay from the hillside and is the house's greatest feature, which made up for the fact that our living quarters were basically all in one room.

I couldn't wait to get inside to cuddle up with Greg, but I still needed to unwind and I hoped he had thought to buy me beer. I was sure he had, even though he rarely drank himself, since he was always thoughtful when it came to me.

Greg, a former Olympic athlete, worked out every morning at sunrise so, by the time I got home that evening, he was dead to the world. I quietly walked down the stairs and through the heavy iron gate which guarded the castle door and provided a safe haven from the world outside.

There was no separation between the kitchen and the bedroom, so it was impossible to turn on a light without waking Greg. As I felt my way through the shadows, my eyes slowly adjusted to the dim light shining through the set of three large, bare windows which overlooked the coast, and I found my way

to the small fridge under the bar.

Because I was trying to be quiet, everything seemed ten times louder than normal. Between the creaking floorboards, the vacuum seal on the refrigerator door, and the hiss of the bottle top, I was certain Greg's eyes would snap open at any minute. I thanked whatever dream held him fast asleep. I pulled a chair up to the center window, leaned back, propped my feet on the sill and let the sound of the ocean transport my mind to faraway places.

My friends often commented on how lucky we were to live at the beach, but with our demanding schedules, neither of us had much time to enjoy it, so sitting in the dark was a special moment for me and turned out to be one I would never forget.

MOON OVER MALIBU
Summer 1988

Dear Diary:

ast night I sat at the window, counting the stars to pass the time. As I began to relax, my eyes kept returning to a particularly bright star low on the horizon. Something about it was different. Perhaps it wasn't a star at all. It could have been a sailboat, although it certainly seemed to be above the water, not on it. As I pondered the possibilities, the mystery star shot across the horizon with breathtaking speed and stopped abruptly at Point Dume. I was amazed by its velocity! Palos Verdes, where the light had been hovering, is roughly forty miles south of Point Dume, yet the point of light covered that distance in a matter of seconds.

I knew I had just observed something literally out-of-this-world! No manmade object could have moved that fast. I wanted to jump up and wake Greg, but I couldn't take my eyes off the bright light and I knew that by the time he got to the window, it would have been gone. What a shame I had to witness such an extraordinary event alone.

As though it responded to my thoughts, the brilliant point advanced until it became a luminous sphere some fifty feet in diameter. It ominously hung in the air less than one hundred feet from my window. I couldn't move, I couldn't scream, I

couldn't breathe. I didn't know if I was about to see God or the Devil himself.

The apparent standoff lasted no more than a minute before the sphere departed as quickly as it appeared. It tore away diagonally through the night sky and vanished. ❤

On the morning of "Rude Awakening," after recalling the incident of the "moon" over Malibu, I walked away from the window and took a very hot, very long shower. I stood numb, listening to the spray beat against my muddled brain. The water felt like tears from heaven weeping with me as I watched my happy life slip down the drain.

My neat little universe had just cracked, and all my years of college hadn't prepared me to confront the ignorance in which I had hidden. My head had not only been ripped out of the sand, it had been taken off, rearranged, and put on backwards.

I felt like an animal raised in a cage, released to an outdoors it had never known. The denizens of the wilderness were so alien, one look into their feral eyes had stripped me of all my defenses. The savage insensitivity of those glacial pits breached the shield that had protected me from my own naivete.

But life, with its impartial attitude, refused to pause for my fear and I was forced to continue with business as usual. Luckily, another "self" showed up and took care of the job of

Moon Over Malibu

living my life. I believe I was in shock for quite some time. I walked around in a trance, feeling nothing but raw vulnerability when *their* callous faces would sneak back into my mind.

That week, I was working as the still photographer for a video of Shalane McCall, a former actress on the TV series *Dallas*. The shoot was not more than a few days into production but I had already become friends with the producer, Gary, a good-looking young man with a gentle manner, whom I liked instantly. He had recently moved to Los Angeles from Missouri, my home state, so we had a lot in common.

When I walked onto the set, the day of my terrible "dream," I tried to act normally, but I was carrying my nightmare on my face. The moment Gary saw me he gasped, "God, what happened to you?"

I stammered, not knowing how to respond. "Wha...what makes you say that?"

"No offense, but you look like hell," he commented.

"Nothing is wrong."

"I know you're lying. Now just tell me what happened and maybe I can help you."

"It's nothing, really...I don't know. Well...I guess I had a very bad nightmare last night and I didn't get much sleep after that."

"So let's talk about it and try to figure out what it meant."

He was so concerned, I felt I had to tell him the truth. We ducked away into a dark corner of the studio, and I began to

recount the event that had occurred less than five hours before. Gary sat quietly, listening to my every word with a very unusual expression on his face. When I finished, he took my hand in his and silently stared into my eyes, like a doctor about to tell a patient she is suffering from a terminal disease and doesn't have much time left.

"Kimberly, there is something I have to tell you." My stomach tightened at the news I was about to hear. "What happened to you last night was not a dream." I wanted to bolt out of the room and run away from his words, but Gary tightened his grip.

I protested, "Of course it was! What else could it have been?"

"Okay, let's say for now that it was a dream. But, if it was, then there are thousands of other people having the same nightmare."

My mind was frantic, and I wasn't whispering anymore, I was almost yelling. "What are you talking about? How would you know anyway?"

"Calm down, this isn't something I can explain to you now. Stay here today, don't worry about the photography, just take it easy. We'll leave early tonight and I'll explain the whole thing to you over dinner. Okay?"

The fight went out of me. "All right."

That evening, Gary and I went to Tommy Tang's, a Thai restaurant on Melrose, another night that shall remain etched in my memory forever. Gary proceeded to tell me about the phenomenon known as "alien abduction," something he learned

about after his roommate suffered a similar ordeal.

Whatever makes up the core of my person was taking quite a beating. I felt my thoughts and emotions tumbling and crashing against one another, like tangled seaweed in a churning tide.

I tried to concentrate on the information Gary was imparting to me, but I was too fascinated with placing every grain of rice exactly the same distance from the other ones on my plate. Despite my resistance, a single tear ran down my cheek and reflected all my feelings of helplessness.

"Doctor" Gary continued to tell me all the terrifying details of my illness. He explained that not much was known about the "disease." No one knew its source, how it manifested, how to identify the symptoms or why it struck certain individuals. The phenomenon seemed to be contagious and was affecting more and more people around the world. Experts in many fields denied the reality of alien abduction, so there was no place to go for help, and most people who had it didn't talk about it because of fear of ridicule.

After dinner, Gary escorted me to the Bodhi Tree, a metaphysical bookstore in West Hollywood, and bought me the paperback *Missing Time* by Budd Hopkins. "Read this," he insisted. "Then we'll talk some more."

I spent the next two days glued to the pages of the book in absolute disbelief. *Missing Time* is a compendium of other people's stories all paralleling my own. A strong shift occurred in my consciousness as I toyed with the idea that what had

happened to me had been absolutely real. The shock slowly gave way to contemplation and finally relief. It was my universe that had cracked, not me!

That night, I wrote Budd Hopkins a ten-page, handwritten letter describing my episode of a few nights prior. Budd kindly responded to my call for help with a long form letter that acknowledged my experience. It also listed resources of where to find help and included a cover page cautioning me of the dramatic impact further research of this event would have on my life.

The next couple of days I fixated on the letter, rerunning it over and over in my mind. The third day, I pulled the letter from my desk drawer and tore it to shreds. That was the end of it for me. It happened…it was over…and I would go on with my life as normal. Or so I thought!

The next two years my life appeared great to all outside observers. I was learning how to maneuver in the freelance world of photography. I had developed the specialty of hand painting my fine art photographs and was doing quite well.

Greg, who was already an award-winning filmmaker, had worked his way through high school and college as a lifeguard on the Southern California beaches, and he had the idea that the thousands of rescue stories on file at the lifeguard headquarters

would make great material for a television series.

NBC thought so, too, and *BayWatch* had its first year as an NBC production.

Our lives changed dramatically. Greg has many talents and beyond creating the series, he was involved as a producer and director. I became the still photographer for the show, and was also able to use my fine art photographs of lifeguard towers as set pieces and background plates for the end-title credits.

We left "the Pink Castle" in Pacific Palisades and moved to Malibu. Now there was nothing between our front door and the water but sand; no more roar of the Pacific Coast Highway. Instead, there was the crashing of the waves which was even louder than the traffic. The constant pounding was the price we paid for such a rare front yard.

But the undercurrent of alien contact was growing stronger and I was having a hard time sharing Greg's excitement and newfound success. Life tugged in two opposite directions, though the power and influence of the glamorous Hollywood lifestyle wasn't much of a match for the mystery of the strange encounters of the night. Greg was being drawn to the bright lights, while I was being drawn deeper and deeper into the darkness of abduction.

As the nightmares came, I stuffed them into the closet of my subconscious. However, the closet was full and for the sake of my sanity, I could no longer conceal the truth from myself.

SEARCHLIGHT
September 29, 1990

Dear Diary:

'm afraid my deepest fears have just been confirmed. I have read a few books that state abduction is an ongoing occurrence in a person's life. Over the last few years, I have refused to acknowledge the strange "dreams" and suspicions I've had, to the point I stopped writing in my diary, but after last night I can no longer stay in denial.

By putting this experience to paper I am admitting I know the truth: I went to bed as usual but suddenly woke up in the middle of nowhere, naked and lost. I was running through a thicket of trees, barely escaping a blinding light which stabbed down from the blackness overhead.

My blood was fueled with adrenaline, and I moved with the instinct of a wounded animal hunted by a pack of ravenous wolves.

The night air stung my skin and my lungs threatened to burst, but I knew I couldn't stop. I feared the invisible power that had unleashed the light searched for more than my body: I was certain it was after my soul.

The next thing I knew I was back in my bed, wide awake, my racing heart reminding me I was better off not remembering until I die if they *got what they came for.*

What in the universe could provoke such terror? I have never believed in a Devil, but now I think I am dealing with something far worse, and why does it have its sinister eyes on me? I can't remember a time I have felt so alone. Please God, let this be just another bad dream! 👽

I succumbed to the disturbing and unfortunate fact that I was involved in ongoing bouts with these creatures of the dark and this really opened up a can of worms for me. Where did they come from, and how often? What manner of evil were they engaged in that required such stealth? Most importantly, who was *I* that the aliens would go to so much trouble to maintain such secrecy?

The questions stacked high. My quest for the truth had begun, but things became a lot worse before they became better. As a matter of fact, my "roller coaster ride from hell" lasted several years before I found any significant answers.

The acknowledgment of my powerlessness threw me into depression. The prowlers obviously had the ability to snatch me from my bed in the dead of night without anyone knowing, including me. They could be (and by their secrecy, probably were) performing any number of unimaginable acts upon my body and mind, and nothing could stop them.

I functioned in the outside world, but I was completely severed from it. My mind was totally obsessed with the unbelievable possibility aliens were silently, secretly controlling the world,

Searchlight

even if only *my* world. I was forced to reevaluate all the philosophical conclusions I had formed. A lifetime of concerted effort to resolve the age-old wonder of the meaning of life left me without a tool to understand this new phenomenon. I thought I had thoroughly digested information on every major religion, but had apparently missed something...something enormous. Where was the book on these nocturnal kidnappers with unlimited power? How did they fit in?

I was beginning to think everything I had ever learned was a lie. If all religion had been designed as a cosmic joke to keep the Earthlings unaware, the makers were successful. The world looked artificial and I couldn't believe people were walking around as if everything was all right. It seemed the entire human race was hypnotized and I desperately wanted to wake them up. Try as I might, nobody cared.

A good friend said, "So what if there are aliens, people lived through the Holocaust, didn't they?" End of discussion.

That aliens were interacting with us in this covert manner was the most disturbing thought I had ever entertained. But, I realized it wasn't a problem for anyone else because it hadn't happened to them. Or so they thought! I would sympathetically observe my friends and colleagues, wondering which of them would one day have "rude awakenings" of their own.

As the months passed, I became an embittered soul. I had spent most of my life as an agnostic, but I was beginning to wonder if there wasn't something to the Christian concept of

Lucifer after all; only a Prince of Darkness could beget beings as demonic as the aliens. I then decided I hated God altogether for allowing the aliens' existence, and finally graduated to, once again, discounting the "God" concept completely. The universe was reduced to the microcosm of planet Earth: a jungle of survival, predator and prey.

I was very satisfied with this deduction for quite sometime. If life was nothing more than random selection and only the strong survived, it was time for me to take my power back.

My anger grew more powerful than my fear. I would confront the silent thieves who had stolen my faith, my security, my stability, and my sleep.

I decided to call them. Every night when I crawled into my "crypt" I would send out a mental message: "I know you are out there, come visit me face to face! I can handle it, if you can!"

This nightly challenge went on for several months and became a habit as the phrase "Now I lay me down to sleep" was when I was a child. "Keep me safely through the night" …what a laugh! But my new prayer did work…finally!

journey

CHICKEN LITTLE
September, 1991

Dear Diary:

I spent last night restlessly tossing and turning, my intuition screaming at me that something was wrong. Finally, my sixth sense alerted me that they *were coming. I was immediately overwhelmed with emotion. I don't know which one was stronger, fear or exhilaration.* They *had apparently received the telepathic messages I had been sending and, to my astonishment,* they *were answering.*

I heard my heart pound and my body stiffened. I didn't know what to do! My yearning to understand them drove me like an addiction, and yet they absolutely terrified me. After several minutes of tortuous dilemma, my curiosity won out. I had to meet them!

I quietly snuck out of the bedroom to keep from waking Greg. The living room was drained of all color and bathed in a faint electronic glow like a late night, black-and-white episode of The Twilight Zone.

I don't know how my trembling legs supported me as I peeked out over the water, wanting to see something, while at the same time hoping I would not. I barely recognized the ocean I had loved for so long; it was dark and threatening. A few silent moments passed before a crack of light shot across

Chicken Little

the water and a rush of wind blew in through the open sliding glass door. Before I could react, a huge, bright, metallic disk magically appeared and hovered inches above the patio fence. I fell to the floor and crawled backwards into the nearest corner. My face flushed and burned, not from fear, but from sheer humiliation at my own reaction. They waited a moment, and I sensed a reassuring message being projected from the craft. We all knew I wasn't ready.

The ship disappeared as quickly as it had come. I was so disappointed in myself for losing such an incredible opportunity, but it was still an amazing occurrence. The aliens didn't seem like monsters anymore. Well, not as much. I was deathly afraid of them and yet they came at my request. To me that seemed like an act of love. At least, I wanted it to be. 👽

The following night I "dreamt" I was with a group of humans on the beach in front of our house. The aliens had returned. After meeting with the group, the aliens took me back into my living room where they projected a series of hieroglyphs onto the wall. Though I could not read the glyphs, I was thrilled the visitors had come back and were trying to communicate with me.

My whole life I've heard people say, "If you die in your dreams, you really die," and my whole life I knew they didn't know what they were talking about.

I have died in my "dreams" more times than I can count. Each time was a variation on the same theme. Without exception, they involved water...

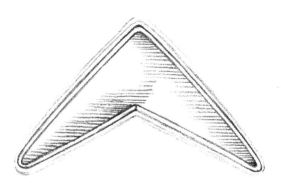

FLUID TRANSITION
October 6, 1991

Dear Diary:

I had another haunting "dream" about breathing liquid. This time, I woke up in a murky ocean. Peering through the cloudiness above my head, I searched for the hidden presence that kept me submerged. It was strange that in the face of death I was completely calm when I should have been panicking.

My burning lungs begged me to inhale and end their agony. I finally let go. As the water poured into my lungs, my spirit rushed out of my body and rose to the surface of the ocean. From that vantage point, I was looking back down at my body and the realization hit me...I was still alive and so was my body, even though I wasn't in it! 👽

In the many other "dreams" I'd had in the past, I assumed that I had died when my essence left my corporeal form. Unconsciously, these experiences influenced my philosophical growth. At a very early age, I already understood the relationship between the spirit and the material worlds.

This time, I looked back and realized my astral and physical bodies were both animate.

Fluid Transition

Recently discovered in my abduction research is "the pool experience," a commonly reported procedure performed by the aliens, now referred to as the "Greys." (That name was probably chosen because of their skin pigment, but it more appropriately describes their emotionless personalities). People are forced into large tanks and left until they have no choice but to inhale, at which point they are happily surprised when their lungs continue to breathe after filling with liquid. The reason for this is unknown.

Perhaps the aliens know impending death releases the soul from the body, and this is one way to help bring about a greater spiritual awareness in the human race: giving us a taste of the larger reality of our being. Then again, the idea the aliens might be here for *our* benefit may be only wishful thinking on my part.

After "Fluid Transition," I did not wake up but went on "dreaming..."

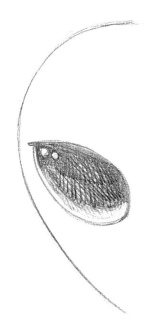

Beyond My Wildest Dreams

HOW DO YOU SPELL ZETA?
October 6, 1991

Dear Diary:

heard a voice call out each individual letter:

Z
ZE
ZET
ZETA
ZETA R
ZETA RE
ZETA RET
ZETA RETI
ZETA RETIC
ZETA RETICU
ZETA RETICUL
ZETA RETICULU
ZETA RETICULUM!

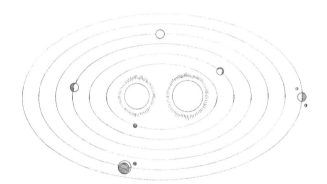

I woke up so abruptly I knew it was intentional. They *did it, to insure I would not forget this message.* 👽

Spell 'Zeta'

I've heard some researchers believe the Grey aliens originate from the binary star system called Zeta Reticulum. This "dream" seems to be a deliberate confirmation that the Greys are "Zetas" from a relatively close planet. Zeta Reticulum can only be seen from the Southern Hemisphere and is approximately thirty-eight light years from Earth. Alleged "Top Secret" documents have revealed information imparted to our government by the Greys which states that their home world is the fourth planet from their sun.

The combination of something trying to drown me and a voice chanting "Zeta Reticulum" in my ear was extremely disturbing. More and more I avoided sleep. Greg loved to retire to the mindlessness of late night TV, while I needed to be completely mentally absorbed to block any and all thoughts of abduction. Thanks to the "Zetas," I became extremely well read. I couldn't go to bed without a book in one hand and a beer in the other. Eventually, even that tranquilizing twosome failed. My nights gave new meaning to the malady of insomnia.

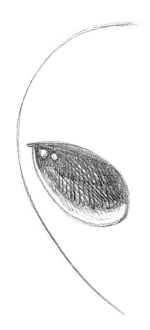

Beyond My Wildest Dreams

"PIER" PRESSURE
October 10, 1991

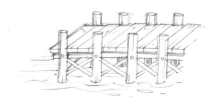

Dear Diary:

I was pulled from the false sanctuary of sleep by a now-familiar foe…terror! A chill of fear ran up my spine at the pressure of an alien's fingertips gripping the bridge of my nose. But the physical pressure was insignificant next to the force of the being's mind as it penetrated my skin like mental novocaine, pushing me into oblivion.

The next thing I knew, my shivering body was clothed only in goose bumps as my bare feet slapped against the cold, sea-soaked planks of a weathered ocean pier.

Moonlight pierced the rippling water, illuminating a half-dozen human figures seated in a circle ten feet below the surface. A powerful resonance swept around me like a rogue wind, delivering a pronouncement of doom: "One of the members of the group is leaving, it is time for you to fill his space."

I fought the voice's command and remained frozen to the spot, staring in horror and disbelief at the sunken congregation. When a frightening white shadow loomed up from the depths near the group, I cried out for understanding, but no one answered.

Kicking and screaming, I fought against the aliens' control as they returned me to bed. Greg, startled from his sleep, had to

Pressure

*wrestle me to the mattress. After several panic-filled moments,
I eventually relaxed into the accustomed ambience of our bedroom, allowing my experience to cloak itself in the guise of a
less threatening, but nevertheless disquieting dream.* ☻

After years of secrecy, I couldn't remain silent any longer.
I had to tell Greg, but how? His father a doctor and his mother
a housewife, Greg had been raised with the conservative views
of traditional Catholicism. I had my work cut out for me.

I started mentioning the night visions and how they seemed
so real. I commented on how unlikely it was we were the only
beings in the universe, but I could see the words fly right over
Greg's head as he responded, "You're probably right, Eddy (my
nickname), so let's have pasta for dinner."

One week I brought home a different UFO film every night
from the video store to gauge his reactions; he finally got irritated.
There was just no room in his understanding for such nonsense
and I certainly couldn't blame him. There wasn't any room in
mine either, but I didn't have the luxury of indifference.

Even if Greg had been interested, it wouldn't have mattered.
His career had consumed his life. The few hours he was home
during the week, he was on the phone with two or three calls
waiting. He went nonstop month after month. The bigger
BayWatch became, and the more I talked about abduction, the
further away he drifted. But I couldn't stop myself, and I certainly

could not change his priorities.

I followed any and all hints that led to more understanding of the night crawlers and discovered the UFO underworld while sniffing around occult bookstores. In the metaphysical world, people seemed to speak openly and acceptingly about the subject of alien encounters, and I started hearing stories more fantastic than my own. But I still had to sift through volumes of bizarre material to find the more believable UFO literature, and even that was buried among conspiracy theories, end of the world warnings, and so on and so on. I developed an extremely keen and discerning eye. Surprisingly enough, the more I learned, much of the nonsense I laughed at in my earlier digs started showing suspicious validity; such as the story that our government is hiding crashed saucers in underground facilities. I became totally immersed in the "New Age" movement. In that open-minded community, I found acceptance when I spoke of the strange events I had witnessed. Not only were people genuinely interested and compassionate, they also already believed the visitors were real, and I could get straight into deeper philosophical discussions on the meaning of the phenomenon. I found that many people who believed in UFOs also engaged in esoteric practices and acknowledged telepathy and other paranormal abilities without question.

My alien contacts proved to me ESP exists and is common, so when I came across the concept of "channeling" I accepted it quite naturally. Channeling is the ability to telepathically

receive communication from other forms of consciousness that are most often nonphysical...in other words, modern-day mediumship.

I felt a telepathic linkup with the Greys many times before they actually arrived and abducted me. I had experienced my soul separated from my body. I didn't need to be convinced of the spiritual realm or that telepathy was possible. Channeling seemed a logical combination of the two.

One day, a friend of mine handed me a flyer regarding a channeling conference in Greece. I thanked her for the flyer and stuffed it in my purse but didn't give it a second thought. I had been to Greece and the trip was thousands of dollars more than I had to spare at the time.

A short while later I had a dream...I was in Greece with all my friends, having the time of my life. An unexpected check had arrived in the mail which had been enough to cover the trip, with spending money left over.

The next day the fantasy badgered me until I finally rummaged through my desk and found the wrinkled flyer. Without reading it, I immediately called the number at the bottom of the page. "Can you tell me anything about this channeling conference in Greece?" I asked.

A female voice responded, "Why, yes! It's really lucky you called, today is the last day to register for that trip. The five-hundred-dollar deposit has to be in the office by five o'clock this evening."

Embarrassed, because I knew I couldn't afford it, I quickly ended the conversation by telling her I'd think about it.

I went about my day, running typical errands, which included picking up my mail at the post office. I thumbed through the pile of junk flyers looking for the important stuff: bills. There were plenty of those, but there was also an envelope postmarked New York with a name I didn't recognize. As I opened it I almost fainted. It was a check for thousands of dollars from a client I thought had stiffed me over two years earlier. The letter said they had been sending the check to the wrong address all that time and they'd finally gotten it straightened out.

I drove home dazed and confused. There were a million things I wanted to do with that money, but I knew a higher power was at work and I wasn't going to challenge it. I called the travel agency and booked the flight.

The Los Angeles International Airport was bustling as usual with business travelers and excited vacationers. Foreign faces and languages flashed throughout the terminal.

I stepped into a ticket line and asked the first person I saw if I was in the right place for the group tour to Greece. A woman with the most beautiful long, wavy brown hair responded, and we struck up a conversation and a friendship.

Joanie would be the first person in the outside world to

whom I would openly confess my secret.

As we boarded the aircraft, I recognized the face of Darryl Anka, one of the "celebrity" channels with the conference. I had seen him in action once, and I was so impressed I just had to tell him. "Hi, you don't know me, but I spoke to you briefly at one of your channelings, and I just wanted you to know how much I enjoyed it."

I suspected he was probably numb to compliments by then, but it turned out he was warm and receptive and I was really taken by him. Another instant bond was formed. Darryl, Joanie, and I filled every minute of the transcontinental flight with heated conversations covering all aspects of channeling, consciousness, and of course, UFOs. The three of us were inseparable the entire trip, and it indeed turned out to be the best vacation of my life.

I didn't know it then, but in Darryl I found a person who truly had knowledge and insight into the whole UFO phenomenon. Darryl would be instrumental in helping me make sense out of my experiences, not to mention he would become one of my best friends.

During that week in Greece, there was a temporary shift in the quality of my contacts. It could have been coincidental, but I prefer to call it synchronicity.

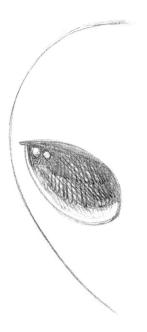

Beyond My Wildest Dreams

"TAKE ME TO YOUR LEADER"
October 18, 1991

Dear Diary:

*N*ormally, when waking from sleep in the middle of the night, my eyes would take in the darkness of my bedroom and the gentle luminescence of the moonlight on the water only yards from my window.

This time, a bright blast of light forced my eyes open. I was walking through a sea of glowing mist, accompanied by an entourage of diminutive grey beings.

Astonished that my consciousness and my control were left intact, I savored the opportunity to observe every little detail and commit them to memory. The aliens felt like children at play around me. They exuded a sense of lightness and a buzzing curiosity that made them appear smaller and less threatening than before.

I realized this moment of lucidity was rare and might not last, so my heart leapt at the chance to make its desire known: to ask the burning question of who, or what, had the authority to dominate my nights. I blurted out the first thing that spilled from my subconscious and demanded that they take me to their leader. It was a line right out of the cheesiest science fiction movie, but it had the necessary effect: it got their attention.

For a moment, everything stopped. The buzz of curiosity

Leader

turned into an air of agreement. We all did an about face and we were "off to see the Wizard."

The vapor dissipated as we approached a towering set of double doors. The doors parted majestically and my mind plunged into blackness.

I regained consciousness as I approached the same doors from the opposite side. My request had been granted but it was obviously deemed important that my interlude with the Greys' suzerain remain wrapped in a cocoon of forgetfulness.

I was navigated back through the fog to the shores of my native reality. Even though I retained only remnants of my exchange with the leader, my relationship with the aliens had been transformed. For the first time in months, I felt at peace.

My world jelled around me and I drifted into the deep, trouble-free sleep of the blessedly innocent. ♥

The little Greys who escorted me to their leader all looked the same and acted in unison; they seemed like nothing more than automatons, the robotic appendages of a vast, mass-mind…a "hive" mentality.

An earthly analogy might be a beehive, where worker-drones, soldiers, and nurses minister to the needs of the queen, all acting under the dominion of a unified consciousness.

Shortly after returning from Greece, I went into surgery. I have had tremendously painful female problems my entire

life. On the days of my cycle, the pain was, and still is, so bad that I am completely incapacitated for three to six days a month. I have tried everything to cure these problems. I went from doctor to doctor in my youth. One doctor was sure it was in my head.

The next one was more compassionate. He said, "I want you to take this baseball bat and hit your old doctor in the shin. When he screams, you tell him the pain is in his head." I loved that doctor, but as understanding as he was, he couldn't help me either, other than prescribing the strongest medicine available. I eventually gave up on doctors and started seeking help in the alternative medicines.

Acupuncture, herbs, psychic healers; you name it, I tried it. Greg, being the son of a doctor, eventually became annoyed with my metaphysical approaches to healing and so did I. Nothing was working, and we decided exploratory surgery was the only thing left.

It was a very traumatic decision for me. I live in Southern California where a woman's worth is determined by her physical perfection, and the man I lived with produced a television series on the beach. Beautiful bodies continually flowed through Greg's office, begging for a part on *BayWatch*. Having my stomach cut in four places for exploratory surgery was the last thing I wanted, but I had run out of choices.

Even worse, I have always had a tremendous fear of doctors, needles, and anything to do with the medical profession, which

I've since learned are the most typical phobias of abductees.

The surgery was performed at one of the best hospitals in Los Angeles by a highly regarded doctor. The surgeon said he found nothing more than a slight case of endometriosis (inflammation of the uterine lining, which he removed). He assured me everything would be better because, in addition, he had severed the nerves to my uterus, cutting off the message of pain to my brain. Unfortunately, the surgery was unsuccessful.

In the following months, the pain was as bad as ever and sometimes worse. I had exhausted about every known method of healing. I resigned myself to the fact I had no other choice but to continue numbing myself with drugs for the remainder of my childbearing years.

The weeks following the surgery, I stayed in bed recuperating, so I had a lot of time to "dream..."

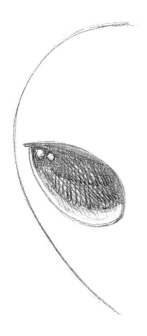

Beyond My Wildest Dreams

"MY, WHAT BIG EYES YOU HAVE!"
November 14, 1991

Dear Diary:

I sat up suddenly after seeing two large eyes floating over the bed. They were probably each one foot in diameter. I have no idea what this meant.

"YOU ARE US"
November 17, 1991

Dear Diary:

The eyes returned. I felt them stare deep within me and a voice spoke a phrase that chilled my very core: "YOU ARE US." I had a startling and profound experience, a realization, a knowing we are all one…one consciousness, one mind, one being! I have never felt anything to be more genuine than that moment. I guess I had a "religious experience," but why do I feel this had something to do with the Greys? That doesn't make any sense, or maybe I don't want it to.

The Eyes

I awoke later that night, floating above the bed where my body lay sleeping next to Greg. I was frightened by the feeling of hands clutching at my head and shoulders, so I escaped back into my body.

"LOOK INTO MY EYES"
November 20, 1991

Dear Diary:

The mysterious eyes have returned a third time. Each experience is more profound than the last. They loomed uncomfortably close as if to physically emphasize the telepathic message they gave me. There was such conviction and urgency behind their words.

"You now see how important it is that we start honoring Earth and repairing the damage we have done. It is time to save Mother Earth from her inhabitants!"

The eyes vanished. I quickly sat up and remained in the dark for hours trying to recall what had happened before the eyes spoke, but my memory had been sealed.

I know I had been given information moments prior to seeing the eyes and even though I cannot consciously remember the details, the eyes were telling me I had inherited knowledge of

great importance and that there's something I'm suppose to do with it. I also received an underlying intimation which suggested by "coming out" about my abductions, the urgency to be more conscious concerning the environment might be felt by a few more people.

I immediately fell asleep and met with this confirming metaphor.

THERE IS NO ESCAPE
November 20, 1991

Dear Diary:

I was an inmate escaping with another female prisoner. We were spotted by a female guard and the woman I was with approached the jailer as if to surrender, but instead snapped the guard's neck. I turned my head and covered my face to shield myself from the senseless murder.

When the imagery ended, a voice took over. "If an unthinkable act is taking place and you turn your head in denial, you are still guilty and responsible."

I stirred as if I had been physically shaken. Somebody or something was determined I would remember this analogy, and I knew it was an exclamation point to the declaration from the "eyes." 👽

I'd heard jokes made many times about space brothers coming here to save us from ourselves, and I'd always laughed. But this time I wasn't laughing. This was one of the most serious moments of my life. I realized I was a lot worse off than I had anticipated. All of a sudden, this wasn't about poor little old me and my abductions anymore. It had instantly transformed into an issue of not only global but universal concern, and I was scared out of my wits. If it was so bad here on Earth that extraterrestrials were coming to employ *me* to help...wow, we must really be in trouble.

As much as I wanted to be able to help the aliens "save the world," I believed they had chosen the wrong person for the job. I was merely an average Joe with less than average influence in the world. I couldn't even hold my own life together; it was crumbling fast.

The day of my surgery, I received a wound no doctor could heal. Greg had been unable to take me to the hospital because he was so tied up with his TV series. Nothing in our relationship had ever hurt me so deeply and I realized I wasn't a priority to him anymore. He had a mistress named *BayWatch* with whom I couldn't compete.

I was so depressed about my health and with this whole new pressure the "dreamlords" had just dumped on me, my

mind warped.

As a result, one day on the set I blew up at Greg. It was one of the ugliest days of my life. To make a long story short, that night I left Greg.

I took my broken heart, my aching body, and my befuddled brain and moved into a little one-bedroom apartment in the Marina. Greg and I continued to date for another year trying to make our relationship work, but unfortunately the aliens had stacked the cards against us.

Darryl and I started spending a lot more time together because we had the same interest: UFOs! We created a couple of projects on the subject, and because we were together so much, Darryl was around when I experienced my physical pain. He was very concerned and suggested I should go to a hypnotherapist because he suspected my medical problems were abduction related. I couldn't see how the two could be related, and I didn't follow his suggestion.

Every couple of months he would bring up the subject of hypnotherapy again, and I would dismiss the idea over and over, until one day I thought the pain was going to kill me. "Okay, I'll try hypnosis," I surrendered, "but I can't go to just anyone. Where will we find someone who believes in this stuff?"

Once again I found myself at the Bodhi Tree bookstore. Darryl and I searched through shelves of UFO magazines and books until we came across the name of a UFO organization, The Center for UFO Studies (CUFOS). With a name like that, they could surely help us.

The next day I called the center and a kind man spent an hour with me on the phone. His name was Mark, and he was so sensitive and caring I will never forget him. He gave me the phone number of a hypnotherapist in Los Angeles who "specialized in abduction hypnosis." My head spun! Not only did he know someone who "believed," he knew someone who "specialized!" All of a sudden I didn't feel like a freak anymore.

Mark also requested I take a series of tests to determine my general psychological profile. I consented, but getting through them was a struggle because the tests were so long and involved. It took several months to complete the questionnaires, and a few more months before I received the scores. However, when the results validated my sanity, I was glad to have taken the effort. In the meantime, I went ahead and called the hypnotherapist.

Yvonne and I spent an evening of getting to know each other at a coffee shop discussing the details of my case. I told

her I wasn't interested in digging up dirt for the sake of curiosity, since I was already conscious through many of my abductions. I sought help because I was searching to understand why I suffered from so much pain. I wanted her to assist me in locating the cause for my physical problems, and nothing more.

She was pleased I had a specific reason and commented that mere curiosity was not a good enough reason for her to work with someone. We set up the appointments.

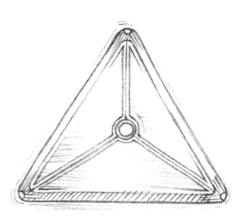

incubation

When I committed to writing this book, it was my intention to transcribe the tapes of my regressions verbatim. I borrowed the tapes from my hypnotherapist and started to listen. What I heard was so disturbing I had to turn the tape player off. My cries of pain were chilling and much too difficult to sit through again. There was so much screaming and sobbing, I doubted even a professional could have transcribed them.

I decided the best route to take would be to rely on my diary notes and memories, which were certainly vivid enough.

"UP YOUR NOSE"
Regression

Dear Diary:

The metal table was ice cold. With all their technology, why couldn't they warm the damn thing up? Green, red, and blue lights flickered in the haze of the examination chamber. A mechanical device suspended a couple of feet above my body scanned the length of my torso. A long tube descended from the ceiling. The aliens attending me shoved the tubing up my right nostril.

I cried out from the pain and begged them for some sort of answer. Why were they torturing me this way? What had I done? They went about their business without offering a scrap of information or a moment of solace.

Time passed in a vacuum. I woke up, still on the table; my arms and legs were strapped to horizontal poles that ran along each side. Three aliens stood around staring at my naked body with their cold, empty eyes.

Another Grey inched closer, carrying something made of glass. I strained my neck to see. That something was a jar containing an alien-like fetus floating in liquid! I didn't dare consider what they planned to do with the grotesque thing.

I struggled against the straps but they ignored me. I could hear their thoughts as they discussed the embryo's gender. As

they brought the bottle closer, I understood what was about to happen. My body was to become its host! I felt trapped in a nightmare far worse than anything I could have ever imagined.

The gruesome scene became even more macabre when a young woman, lingering in the background shadows, hesitantly offered me a wilting rose, as if that was supposed to comfort me. By the look of sheer anguish on her face, I knew she was there against her will just as I was, both of us wondering how we got into such a mess!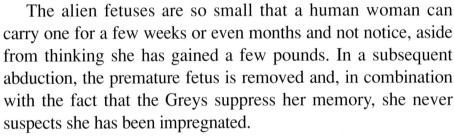

The alien fetuses are so small that a human woman can carry one for a few weeks or even months and not notice, aside from thinking she has gained a few pounds. In a subsequent abduction, the premature fetus is removed and, in combination with the fact that the Greys suppress her memory, she never suspects she has been impregnated.

I believe the hose they inserted in my nose was for the purpose of placing or removing a tracking device. This is one of the most commonly reported medical procedures in other abductee accounts.

There are now several independent efforts under way to remove, study, and catalog the implants which have been found on X-rays and CAT scans, though some implants are located near sensitive areas of the brain and are inoperable. Upon analysis, most objects which have been removed appear to be made of some crystalline-metallic alloy containing recognizable

"Up Your Nose"

elements, but fused together in unusual ways.

The small bead-like implants, used by the Grey aliens, may serve a number of purposes: certainly as homing mechanisms to assist the aliens in locating their prey, and possibly as recording and transmitting devices to eavesdrop on the life of the abductee. They could also be used to raise our cellular vibratory frequency, an adjustment which is needed to make the physical shift into their dimension. Another theory is, the implants may be used to create the paralysis the aliens induce when performing the abductions.

The paralyzing sensation which precedes each abduction is a terrifying experience of total helplessness. The Greys usually wait until the brain waves lower to theta or delta level before intruding. These periods occur during sleep, when we are most susceptible to their manipulation.

I have trained myself to wake up and break free of the paralysis on several occasions, but only when I managed to summon great bursts of emotional energy and will power. This happens most often when I believe close friends might also be in danger of being abducted along with me. The battle of wills sometimes lasts for hours, until the aliens finally concede as dawn robs them of their mantle of night.

FETAL EXTRACTION
Regression

Dear Diary:

The term "ignorance is bliss" most likely came from an abductee. I don't know which is the lesser of two evils, knowing or not knowing what really happened to me. Why couldn't I have remained oblivious?

I think I'm starting to comprehend how much they have taken from me...just when I didn't think it was possible to hate them any more.

The regressions are physically and emotionally painful; I don't know how many more I can take. But at least now I have some of the larger missing pieces of this tortuous abduction puzzle.

Under hypnosis, I actually relived all the physical sensations. I was on a table. A drugged feeling slowly faded as I tried to make sense of the scene that unfolded around me. The Greys' mental communications were urgent and irritable. Something was terribly wrong! I followed their focus down toward my legs which were spread apart. One of the aliens was removing something from between them: an extremely tiny newborn, almost fetal. I heard them say they couldn't stop my bleeding. I also heard my heart cry. Wanting to sleep forever, I begged for death to terminate my grief as I finally drifted back down into a

drug-induced slumber. Now I understand the meaning of the term, "your own private hell" !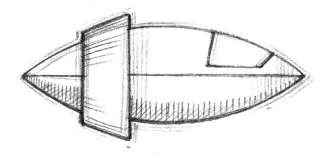

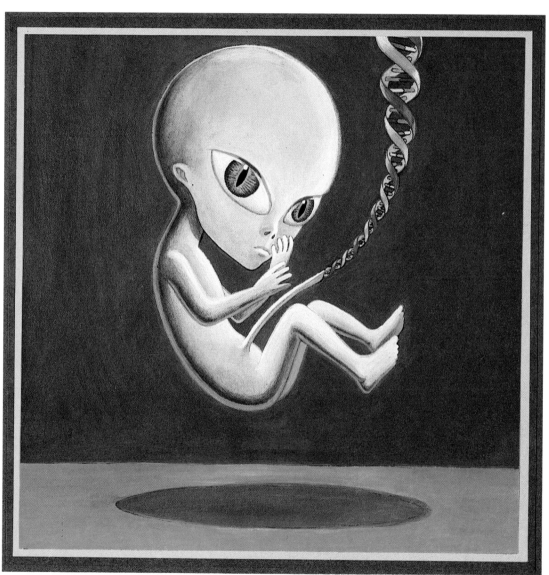

Fetal Extraction

"LOVE THE BABY"
Regression

Dear Diary:

'm sitting on the edge of a stool in a dark room filled with incubation boxes. Two figures in white gowns approach me in silence. I call them the "nurses." They are handing me something. It's so small, I'm afraid to look at it. Oh my God, I'm so scared, I don't want to see its face. They are out of their minds...they're insane...I can't do that! My breasts don't have any milk...it's physically impossible!

They are playing with my mind now. They are trying to get me to be sympathetic. "Love the baby," they chant. "Remember when you were so small and you needed to be loved?" (I was never that small!) I'm holding it now. It's so frail...it's going to die, I know it is, it's too small to live. I can't look at its face, I focus on its feet instead. I can't believe they are making me do this. I have to think about something else...anything else. I put my finger in the arch of its foot, and the tip of my finger fills the entire arch of the foot, that's how small it is! 👽

"Love The Baby"

"ISN'T SHE A BEAUTIFUL BABY?"
February 29, 1992

Dear Diary:

I went to sleep last night and came to as I was ushered by two small Grey beings into an empty room. Although I was twice their size, they effortlessly coaxed me to my knees with their persuasive mental powers. As I scanned the cramped space, a door opposite the one we entered appeared in the far wall.

Three small children, two boys and a girl, scurried into the room accompanied by an alien elder. The female child stopped just beyond my arms' reach and fixed her enormous blue eyes on me with an expectant stare.

My eyes followed the skinny hand of one of my Grey escorts as he presented the child to me in a sweeping gesture of pride. His action and tone were completely out of character as he boasted, "Isn't she a beautiful baby?"

The normally unemotional and increasingly unpredictable Greys radiated a mysterious urgency aimed directly at me. A dim, primal thought aroused my concern, and it dawned on me what they wanted me to realize: this ethereal toddler was quite possibly my own flesh and blood.

I could tell the aliens were waiting in anticipation for the emergence of the natural mother/child bond, even though they

"Isn't She Beautiful?"

couldn't have picked a more unnatural setting.

I was incapacitated by my own distress. I'm not sure if I was unwilling or unable to evoke the feelings required for my participation. The child was foreign to me and I fought against even the slightest connection developing between us, fearing I might become caught up in some manipulative scheme. Or worse, I might have recognized she really was my daughter and have to face the pain of living without her in my life. When they realized I was not willing to cooperate, I was immediately returned to my bedroom. ☻

Well, it didn't take a rocket scientist to get the picture at that point. The regressions were poignant enough, but my tight-lipped friends finally told the whole story in one sentence, "Isn't she a beautiful baby?" That's what all this was about! They are doing the same thing we are doing all over the world: creating offspring. Only theirs are a little more difficult to come by because they are blending two very different species. They don't have the simplicity of nature's way and I could tell by their telepathic expressions it had been a long, hard road to attaining such a perfect specimen.

That little girl, whom I eventually named Aqua after her ocean blue eyes, was indeed beautiful. But as special as she was, there was a coldness to her, though that would not be the case with the others I would eventually meet.

In the days following the "presentation of Aqua," many sad

memories surfaced. They were of other infants I had seen somewhere in my "dreams." Most had been frail and sickly, many on the verge of death. Others were grossly deformed. Even the healthier ones in the nurseries I was "persuaded" to "nurture" were so small I was certain they would not make it. I empathetically understood why the Greys were so elated with that flawless wonder.

I reviewed my life with this new information in mind and many of the strange phobias I never understood became grimly clear. I have always had a deep-seated fear of having children and I refused to ever think about the subject. My friends would ask me why and, as unfounded and illogical as my answer was, I told them the truth. "I'm afraid if I have them, someone will take them away."

Of course, the reason for my aversion to medical procedures was now obvious. The visitors' crossbreeding program has been a process of trial and error, my body suffering many of the errors.

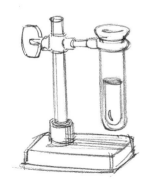

The alien hybridization is quite complex. Their "modus operandi" is to collect sperm and ovum from human beings and combine our genetic material with their own. At this point, the embryo is implanted into the human female to gestate for a short time until she is abducted again and the fetus removed, thus explaining my own bizarre "miscarriages."

It's a mind-blowing prospect no matter how you look at it, but I have heard the aliens quoted as saying, "You do the same

thing to the animals on your planet." Not long ago a friend told me that some dog breeders breed females literally to death. They are impregnated constantly until their bodies are prematurely worn out, then they are killed when they are no longer "productive." I hope the Greys aren't patterning their actions on our own.

I do not know how many times this abhorrent procedure has been performed on my own body, but I realize, with the aliens' techniques, it wouldn't take too many to do serious damage to one's body and soul. They are advanced in some ways, but great doctors they aren't, and when it comes to bedside manners, forget it! Darryl had been correct in assuming my female problems were abduction related. Even though the hypnotherapy didn't cure the pain, I had a better understanding of the problem.

When I began my hypnotherapy with Yvonne, I had agreed to refrain from reading any more material on the UFO/abduction subject so that my own regressions would be unpolluted. I had honored that agreement even though some ground-breaking publications were coming out at the time.

Shortly after my meeting Aqua, several of my good friends from out of town were visiting Los Angeles for the Whole Life Expo. Six of us went out for dinner at a Japanese restaurant in the Marina. I was discussing my experience of having the child presented to me when Darryl interrupted. "Don't say another

word about this until I get back." He excused himself to fetch something from his car and returned with a new research book about abduction entitled *Secret Life* by David Jacobs. Darryl commented, "I know you have agreed to avoid UFO material, but you must see this one sentence." The sentence was a chapter subheading which read, "Isn't she a beautiful baby?"

I didn't know what to say. My imagination went wild. The Greys are obviously using this "line" on many abductees. Are they limited in their vocabulary or are they trying to pull something over on us? Could the truth be the hybrid children are a mishmash of genetics with no particular parents and the aliens are trying to trick us? Or are the children truly from specific bloodlines?

After years of contemplation, I've concluded it is a moot question. The hybrid children need human bonding. They live in a heartless, alien environment where emotion is almost nonexistent. Whether the aliens are keeping track of my specific genetics or not, I have carried these babies in my body; they are helpless and lonely and, when we are brought together, I now give them all the love I can.

Maybe that's what the aliens depend on: the human capacity for love and compassion they are incapable of. The children are not responsible for the ruthlessness of their creation. Perhaps, eventually, this new race will be able to communicate to the Greys how cruel their methods are, since they don't

seem to understand or care at this point. Quite possibly, that is the intention of spawning this new generation: to be the bridge between human understanding and alien intelligence. Because we are so different, these mediators may be required if we are to ever have open exchange with other worlds.

I've conceived countless theories why the hybrids are being born at what seems to be an emergency pace. I've been personally warned by the Greys that our environment is at a crisis point. I recently learned that within the last twenty years, the human male sperm count has dropped by 50 percent.

Maybe the hybrids are a last-ditch effort to preserve the DNA of a dying species. The aliens might be breeding them to replace us, or join us in an effort to save Mother Earth.

Of course, I have heard other theories, such as the aliens destroyed their own planet and lack the ability to reproduce other than by cloning. Perhaps they are using us to fortify their own species. If so, this may be a solution to halt the decline of both worlds.

There is also the possibility our destructive actions are infringing on extraterrestrial turf and the aliens are acting in self-defense. Science is blind to the existence of their dimension, so scientists are certainly unaware of how our realms interact and affect one another. A nuclear explosion on Earth, or even prolonged exposure to radioactive waste, could rip a hole in the dimensional wall, sending a crippling wrinkle through eternity.

Therefore, the urgency of the aliens' genetic program may

well be to insure their own survival by creating a more intelligent race and repopulating Earth before such a disaster occurs.

Or maybe they have been here all along and this planet is nothing more than the breathing sculpture of an extraterrestrial Michelangelo. I have asked them many times for the answer to this question, but so far I have been ignored.

integration

When I needed to fill in some of the gaps of my experiences, hypnosis served as an invaluable tool, and I regret when this method is denigrated by the "almighty scientific community," or it is suggested that people make up their stories with the aid of leading questions by anxious hypnotherapists. My regressions taught me so much about the unconscious, and I have great respect for hypnosis as a viable choice in therapeutic work.

I have had countless extraordinary encounters, and I was fully aware of them for many years before I contacted a hypnotherapist. What came out in the sessions were simply more details of already-vividly-recalled events. Most people who undergo hypnosis for abduction are very much like me. One does not wake up in an ordinary life and say, "Oh, I think I'll go be hypnotized to see if I'm being contacted by aliens!" Seeking healing with the aid of hypnosis is a courageous step in a difficult process of understanding a history of irregular happenings, and I would personally recommend it to anyone who is finally integrating "visitor" experiences. I also believe it should not be undergone without the assistance of a qualified psychologist who is familiar with the abduction phenomenon. Most hypnotherapists are not psychologists. In my opinion, confronting the hidden memories is mandatory for wholeness, but the overwhelming feelings of helplessness that accompany the abductions need to be healed as well.

Close Encounter Research Organization (CERO) is the name of a support group comprised of abductees who have

been through hypnotherapy with Yvonne. When Yvonne feels clients are at a point of understanding in general what is happening to them, they are invited to attend the monthly support group meetings where they can, possibly for the first time in their lives, speak frankly about their experiences to others who understand. The fellowship constantly changes as new people join and old members take breaks, but the comraderie is powerful regardless of the varying faces. Upon meeting fellow abductees, you unmistakably recognize other souls who have been to the "edge." The clenching intensity and knowingness that resides in their eyes establishes instant rapport.

There are also strikingly similar characteristics among people of contact. They are usually deeply philosophical individuals with extraordinary insight and instinct. As a result of my contacts, I have been left with unusual attributes, such as telepathy and hands-on healing abilities. (Unfortunately for me, my healing hands work best on other people.) It was consoling to discover many contactees display powers similar to mine. Humanitarian and ecologically minded, they are not your typical cocktail-party personalities.

As evolved as contactees seem to be in specific areas, they are otherwise very normal people outside of the exclusive UFO fraternity. *I* didn't have a clue about this "other side" of people I had known for years until I started investigating my own experiences.

I had attended regular monthly meetings for some time

when, one Sunday afternoon, as I made my way to the meeting room (Yvonne's dining room), I passed a woman I recognized. She was someone who had been a close associate of Greg's in the past, and I knew her quite well. Allison is one of the sweetest, most unassuming women I have ever met. Needless to say, I was shocked to see her there. Her reaction to my presence was subdued, because she had been informed I was a member weeks before the meeting. I, on the other hand, was unprepared. That was not the place I expected to run into someone I knew.

It had been a safe environment when it was just a roomful of "touched" people I knew nothing about beyond our mutual encounters. As difficult as it was to integrate the knowledge of the "visitors," there were still times I needed my denial. I could escape back into it by avoiding the meetings and keeping my "real" world separate. But there stood Allison, someone from the "outside"; someone I knew well, had worked with on the same show...someone I was certain was not crazy. That confirmation was bigger than I wanted to accept, but an even bigger validation was right around the corner.

At the same time I was frequenting CERO, I would occasionally sit in on MUFON meetings. The Mutual UFO Network gave me a well-rounded view of the UFO phenomena because it is made up of many different types of enthusiasts, not just those experiencing contact. Anyone interested in the subject is welcome: researchers, scientists, psychologists, or simply those who are curious.

Experts in many fields speak on their given specialties. One evening, Yvonne was invited to address the subject of abduction and was asked to bring anyone in her group who wanted to share particular stories. I decided it was time to tell mine, even though it was an extremely frightening decision. Of course, I was concerned I would appear foolish, but more importantly, speaking to the public meant I was convinced of the validity of my own experiences.

The day I was to participate on the panel was a work day and, unfortunately, my shoot ran overtime. I rushed to the meeting, arriving after the first speaker was already engaged at the podium. As I searched the room for my fearless leader, Yvonne waved to me from a table at the back wall where she was seated with the "gang." A woman I didn't recognize, sitting next to Yvonne, reacted strongly to my arrival. The woman grabbed Yvonne's arm, whispered something in her ear, and continued to stare at me as if she was seeing a ghost. I was extremely uncomfortable and looked away, but I could still feel her eyes on me.

At the break, I squeezed through the crowd and Yvonne introduced me to Kathleen, a relatively new client of hers. "Hi, it's very nice to meet you," I said nervously. "Hi, Kim, it's nice to meet you, too, but I already know you!" I studied her face for any familiarity, but there was none.

"What do you mean?" My anxiety heightened.

"Let's just say I've seen you before."

At that point, Yvonne took both of us to the side and said, "We'll discuss this after the meeting, but now we have to go up front." I was taken aback by Kathleen's comment, and I could not believe I was forced to sit with my pressing curiosity for the rest of the evening.

The moment the session broke, I pounced on the woman. "What do you mean you've seen me before?"

She explained, "My experiences have been different from yours."

I was really agitated by then. I knew Yvonne's policy of confidentiality did not permit her to discuss her cases with anyone, and my suspicion grew that Kathleen's knowledge was firsthand. "When I am abducted, I am often forced to observe," Kathleen continued. "The most horrible thing I have ever seen is what I saw them do to you!"

I felt my knees weaken and suddenly there wasn't enough oxygen in the room. A question, seemingly unrelated to the conversation, came to my lips, but I realized that I already knew the answer. "What do you do for a living?"

"I'm a makeup artist."

I wasn't sure I could continue the conversation and was grateful when Yvonne interrupted. "Kathleen came to me several months after you and I started working together. She related to me the same story I had heard you recount but from another point of view. When she told me about the woman 'she would never forget,' she described you perfectly. I did not tell either

one of you and planned this evening to see if she would recognize you in a crowd."

When I regained my composure, Kathleen described seeing me strapped to a table. The Greys were implanting an alien fetus into my body as I writhed in horror. I had one more burning question. "Do you know a man named David G?" I asked. "Why, yes, I do, I know his brother Steven quite well."

That was all I needed to know. My first conscious abduction involved a woman who was a makeup artist and David G. It was almost too much to absorb. As I drove home late that night, I remembered the woman in my regression who held the wilting flower. In my hysteria during that abduction, I had not concentrated on the woman's face, so I wondered if it was her. Maybe sometime in the future I will ask Kathleen how she feels about roses!

My involvement with the aliens had become the most prominent aspect of my life. I was sick of the secrecy and I desperately needed to know more about them. Nothing had ever had such power over me, and I was determined to discover what gave them the right to invade my life. I remembered they had responded to my request to meet them face to face in the earlier part of our "relationship," even though I had "chickened out." Much had gone down between us since then and maybe I

was ready. I started sending out messages again. "I know you are abducting me. The drugs make me sick and it takes days to recuperate from the effects. Let me be conscious, I will cooperate. I won't be a problem, I promise!" My new bedtime mantra went on for about six months before they decided to trust me.

I grew up in the Midwest in a typically dysfunctional family. My father had a problem with alcohol and my mother had a problem with my father.

When my parents would fight, my father would lock my brother and me in a bedroom. To frightened, helpless children, listening to our mother's shrieks was pure hell. I would hide in a corner, cover my ears, and push my consciousness as far away as possible from those ugly confrontations. I would "go inside" so far, so deep, I would escape the screams and the pain. I got very good at it.

Later on in life, while studying psychology in college, I learned my childhood survival mechanism had a name: dissociation. But there was another phenomenon that occurred in those scary times. When I would dissociate, I would hear a voice say to me, "It doesn't have to be this way."

I knew the voice was speaking about the way my parents conducted their lives. Its words carried so much meaning I

don't know how a three-year-old could comprehend them, but I did. The communication foretold of a new way human beings could relate that I would one day understand and own. It explained that my parents and many other people in my world were not innately bad, but they lacked knowledge. Human beings were going to experience an acceleration in evolution, and I would see many changes in my lifetime.

When times were the worst, the voice would come and its message was always the same. "It doesn't have to be this way." As I grew up, the voice came less and less because I had been taught well. Every time I saw a stupid or cruel act, my first thought would be, "It doesn't have to be this way."

This was the strongest belief I carried through life. I knew beyond a shadow of a doubt that personal and global dilemmas could always be solved or improved. There were no such things as problems, only challenges. That one line, and all the meaning that went along with it, was the most powerful gift I ever received, and I never knew where it came from.

Now I suspect it originated from another dimension of knowledge. That little trick of pushing my consciousness inward may have opened the door to a separate reality.

NOT AGAIN
August 8, 1992

Dear Diary:

Night before last I turned in early. I woke up terrified only a few hours later from a stabbing sensation in my abdomen as if something inside of me was battling to escape. My sluggishness suggested a drug was at work in my blood, but my fear overpowered it and I made my way to the bathroom to examine my body.

The evidence of abduction was everywhere. My belly was bloated and smeared with a white powdery substance, and a long red "cat scratch" ran up my right inner thigh. A rope-burn sensation stung my lower back and my breasts were sore and swollen. I stuck my tongue out at the mirror to see a gouge in the middle. I wanted to believe I had just bitten my tongue, but I knew it was an empty wish.

Even though I was panicked, I couldn't fight the drug any longer, so I went back to bed and stayed there.

By afternoon I was starving and the hunger pains forced me to tend to my basic needs, but that's all I could manage. The burning sensation in my abdomen kept me incapacitated the entire day. For a while I comforted myself pretending I didn't know the reason why, but I couldn't fool my body; it was rejecting what had been implanted in it against my will. Even

Not Again

though I was physically worn out and emotionally numb, I could sense the aliens monitoring me. They were as aware of the complications as I was.

By nightfall, still exhausted and desperate for some REM sleep, I unplugged the phone hoping to get some rest, but instead, became hyperalert. The pain in my uterus had increased. As I lay in bed, my right hand moved to my belly as if it had a mind of its own and came to rest where the pain was strongest. At the same time, my left hand rose and rested on my forehead. I tried pulling my hands away but they were held in place as if they and my body both contained internal magnets.

It felt like waves of electricity flowed through my hands and circled from my belly to my head, flooding me with energy. The Greys must have been producing the bizarre phenomenon, even though they weren't visibly present. I lay frozen in that position with my eyes wide open all night. Midnight came and went...2:00 A.M...3:00 A.M. By 4:00 A.M. it became unbearable. I needed to be on the set of BayWatch *by 6:00 and had to rest, if only for an hour. Summoning all my strength, I yelled out for them to stop and broke my hands free. For one moment I thought I had won out, but something immediately told me I was really in trouble.*

STEWART
Conscious Abduction
August 9, 1992

buzzing filled the room. The sound was so intense my entire body vibrated. My eyes locked onto a spot on my closet doors and watched the impossible happen. Four figures passed through the sliding doors as if the doors were smoke. I blinked several times to see if I was hallucinating …no such luck. Then I forced my eyes shut, hoping that would be enough to turn such a queer reality into a dream. I nevertheless peeked between my eyelids with morbid fascination.

They glided like phantoms: two to my head, two to my feet. One pushed his distorted features to within an inch of my nose. "We know you are not asleep," he said, "you asked for this." No wonder someone once told me, "Be careful what you ask for, you just may get it!"

Suddenly our bodies rose weightlessly toward the ceiling. At the same time, I realized I had somehow become telepathically joined to the being on my immediate left. I was overwhelmed with feelings of disgust, but I couldn't tell which one of us was more repulsed by the other.

I pushed my hand against his crowding face, praying some distance would break our mental link. In the struggle for escape, my thumb slipped into the being's mouth and brushed against the hard palate. It was solid, wet, and warm. I realized

this was a living, breathing "ghost" made flesh.

Again, we were one mind, thinking the same thought: "It doesn't have to be this way!" (Where had I heard that before?) Simultaneously, the alien stunned me with an all-too-human gesture: he kissed me!

I marveled in disbelief. I didn't know if it was a trick, or if the being and I actually had feelings for each other. With that thought I knew I was delirious; of course it was a trick! Then another powerful psychic wave filled me with love.

It seemed the combination of the intimate contacts, physical and mental, had cracked the being's stoic veneer, revealing a tenderness I was sure, until that moment, his kind were incapable of. I guess his extraordinary response was due to the recognition that we were more alike than not. Or maybe we already had a relationship deeper than I could ever suspect.

Our compounded emotion intensified and surged through me; I experienced the inevitable effect of the kiss of death: I went completely unconscious. What seemed only seconds later, I was jogged awake by the bouncing of my body upon the surface of a cold metal gurney rolling down a hospital-like hallway. Back to their true nature, my escorts' demeanors were as cold as the table I was lying on, in contrast to the previous moment's ecstasy. Disheartened, I accepted I was now nothing more to them than cargo as they transported me to the next destination.

My naked body was draped in a white sheet, leaving only my head and arms exposed. A tingling sensation in my third eye

Stewart

prompted me to reach for my forehead. To my amazement, it was not my physical hand that moved, it was instead an astral hand that responded. With everything else that was going on, even that didn't seem strange.

Groups of humanoid beings in the halls interacted with other Grey aliens and barely noticed as I was wheeled past. I struggled to take in the surroundings that rushed by, and saw some unfamiliar life-forms which lay motionless on the floor. These beings were soft and shapeless like mounds of bread dough, yet they each radiated a sweet intelligence. I wondered if they were the aliens' equivalent of our canine companions.

As if aliens everywhere wasn't odd enough, the atmosphere itself had "other dimensional" qualities. I also experienced a sense of nonlinear reality, as if continuity of time didn't exist. I was thrust into one scene after another. My consciousness would fade and refocus according to the aliens' desires. It was called forth and banished as easily as one would flick a light switch on and off. I went blank.

When the light of my consciousness returned, the set had changed. I was alone in a long, antiseptic hall. The only thing I recognized was the all-too-familiar anxiety I have come to know as the exclusive signature of abduction. I had somehow freed myself from my bodyguards and was desperately seeking an escape route. Instinct told me the only way out was up, so I looked for an elevator.

Suddenly, my hope for freedom crumbled. I was caught by

their vigilant telepathy. Feeling their closeness like breath on the back of my neck, I immediately swung around to face my fate.

To my surprise, I was confronted by an elderly woman. Authority filled the many lines of her face and the human mask might have been convincing had it not been for the dead give-away of the being's telepathic intrusion.

I swallowed my fear and scrambled my thoughts to keep her at bay, but I could sense her amusement at my awkward attempt to match her telepathic prowess. I felt like a mouse in the paws of a cat, being kept alive just long enough to satisfy its curiosity.

"Where is the elevator?" my thoughts demanded. "The second door," she responded immediately. Feeling victorious, I turned and walked away. I was pretty sure I had fooled her into thinking I was one of her kind, but I could sense she was still "listening," and at that moment my own thoughts were my worst enemy.

I was so absorbed by the task of masking my inner dialogue, I mistakenly reached for the handle of the first door I came to. A thought pierced my mind. "Not that door, the next one." It was her thought. I felt my heart jump to my throat and I stumbled down the hall praying she was not on to me.

As I lunged toward the second door, I felt the pressure of the cold metal handle against my sweaty palm. I wondered if she sensed that, too. While mustering my remaining energy to push through the heavy glass partition, my head instinctively spun

around like a motion detector and caught sight of four Greys moving in on me from the opposite direction. She *had undoubtedly summoned them.*

Some time later, I clawed my way back to semiconsciousness and, with a sickening sense of déja vu, I found myself back on the rolling table. My shadows were back. They were wheeling me through a large door with a horizontal split, and we entered a small, square room. Still drowsy, I couldn't tell if I was in some small, connecting chamber between larger rooms or if it was a large elevator. Nevertheless, the blue quilted fabric that hung on the side wall created the illusion that I was about to be locked in a padded cell.

That notion faded as my attention was drawn to a human face: a breathtakingly handsome male face. His features were so perfect they looked like the handiwork of some divine doll maker. He rose out of a plastic body bag which lay upon a tabletop or large drawer protruding from the wall—a timeless statue preserved in plastic and brought to life by some unseen sorcery.

A kind, disembodied voice called out my name. "Kim, wake up. It's Stewart." When our eyes met, something familiar stirred inside of me. It was a profound recognition of someone I knew intimately, but of whom I had no actual memories.

Murphy's law: If things can get stranger, they will! Instantly, irrationally, I was in love with the being and that thought flooded me with panic. Maybe the Greys had reached

into my secret heart and designed the ideal soul mate they knew I could not resist.

If so, Stewart was only a sophisticated ploy created to take advantage of my hope for a rescuer. I figured once I surrendered to the illusion of safety, my captors would stand back while I fell under my "white knight's" spell, thus perpetuating their diabolical breeding program.

"Wake up, Kim, it's okay. It's me, Stewart, remember?" This was not the cold pressure of the Greys' telepathy. I fought my way to full consciousness and received the man's telepathic reassurance. Although I could find no memory of Stewart and he offered no explanation of our relationship, I was sure he cared about me.

I was filled with an intense longing for him. Whether a real human or just a disguise, as crazy as it seemed, I wanted to be with him forever. Only moments before, I felt entombed in a dungeon, but with Stewart's arrival, I was in heaven.

Then I had a sad realization about the inevitability of our situation. I had been conscious long enough to realize I was dealing with something more complicated than merely being taken by strange beings to a strange place. Stewart's world and mine existed in different realms and once my time there ended, I might find myself back outside "The Looking Glass" again, grasping for the traces of a fading dream.

As if time and space did not exist, the setting changed again. Fully dressed, I stood in a hall across from the man I knew as

Stewart. His head was cocked toward the floor as though he was listening to internal instructions. His attention shifted to me and, with a subtle motion, he reached into a pocket of his lab coat and withdrew a hypodermic needle.

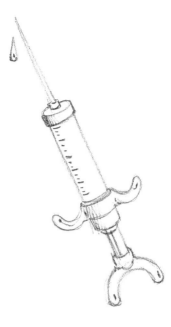

Stewart paused, and with a gentle glance he offered me a choice: it was time to go home, and I could return in the only manner Stewart could provide for me, or I could find my own way back.

Something literally magical happened! Every cell in my body recoiled from the needle's threatening tip and, instantaneously, my consciousness imploded and collapsed into a brilliant point of light. The next moment, with equal intensity, my awareness expanded and my ordinary sense of self returned as my own reality reclaimed me. I had teleported back to my room and was sitting on the edge of my bed! My eyes blinked open. I glanced at my clock: 5:40 A.M.

The Looking Glass had shattered and I came crashing back to this world. My prayers to know the aliens consciously have been answered and a shard of that other realm remains in my memory. I now know Stewart's world coexists with our own, intimately intertwined and separated only by the thinnest veil —our arrogant assumption that we are the sole proprietors of the only reality.

But without the key of passage, the veil is impenetrable. I am sure that key is locked in our consciousness, and I believe I have just scratched the surface of what we call reality. 👽

All I had been through up until "Stewart" had prepared me for anything and, at that point, teleporting from one dimension to another wasn't that surprising, although it was probably the most fascinating thing I've experienced in this life. As a matter of fact, knowing the aliens reside in a different reality explains why this whole UFO phenomenon is so slippery—why it's so difficult to acquire physical evidence or get photographs of their craft. They have the capacity to escape our perception by shifting to an alternate realm.

It is frustrating trying to describe something like another dimension when there is nothing comparable in our domain, but crossing over was as real and distinct as crossing a state line or a nation's border. It was similar to going underwater or out into space...I just went in another direction.

It convinced me we exist within a matrix of many dimensions all merging in one spot: the mind. We don't have to wait until we die to investigate these foreign territories. We can physically explore other realms while incarnate if we desire to pursue such knowledge. But to begin this kind of leap in human consciousness will require a dissolution and restructuring of our beliefs about the nature of reality and the human soul. Perhaps the theory of the hundredth monkey will facilitate that beginning.* I know there are at least ninety-nine "monkeys" other than myself who have taken a ride with the Zetas.

We may be closer than we think. The history of humankind has been punctuated by personalities who refused to be bound

by the grand illusion of space and time. From the Egyptian priests, to the Aborigines and their link to "Dreamtime," to the American Indian shamans, it has been the goal of spiritual seekers to penetrate the limitations of mind and form.

But how are the seeds of curiosity planted so deeply in some that they never rest from their seeking, while so many others live unburdened by an insatiable need to comprehend the mysteries of the universe? Perhaps those seeds are rooted in "dreams."

*The "Hundredth Monkey" hypothesis proposes that once a certain number of individuals have learned a particular item of knowledge, then "critical mass" is sufficient to make that knowledge immediately available to the consciousness of the rest of the group through some form of telepathic connection. This phenomenon was recognized when a small group of monkeys, isolated on an island, had learned to wash sweet potatoes in salt water to make them taste better. It was observed that, once a sufficient number of the monkeys had adopted this habit, suddenly all the monkeys on the surrounding islands started doing it too, even though the islands were separated by dozens of miles and it had never been observed in their behavior prior to that moment despite years of observation.

It has been noted in human society that, once a difficult accomplishment has been achieved, it seems easier for others to achieve, even if no one has reported the initial breakthrough to them.

The Greys have transformed my view and experience of creation beyond words. That does not excuse the violence perpetrated against my body and the disarrangement of my life. My expanded consciousness and mental abilities are merely the outcome of my contacts with them. They are not gifts, per se. That one abduction, sprinkled with a few moments of ecstasy, did not erase all the years of agony I had lived through.

Now I was more familiar with them and certainly the enemy you know is better than the enemy you don't know. I still resented them, but my fear had transformed into concern for the preservation of my body. I knew the physical abuse would continue as long as they were in my life, and as much as ever, I wanted the abductions to stop, but of course the aliens had other plans.

COMPLEX-ITIES
Conscious Abduction
August 30, 1992

Dear Diary:

*B*irthdays aren't what they use to be! My best friend *Catherine and I went out for a quiet dinner and I was home in bed by 10:30 P.M. I slipped under the covers and it hit me. A wave of energy rushed through my body, lifted my left hand to my forehead and glued it there.* They *had been waiting. (How thoughtful of them to remember my birthday!)*

I can't figure out why that thing with the hands happens, but then again I can't figure out why any *of this happens. The familiar sharpening of my senses began and everything in the room, including me, took on an electrical charge. Then I went to the other extreme and passed out.*

They did it again, the old "wake her up in a standing position" stunt. I always feel like the subject of a hypnotist's stage act but I can never find the hypnotist. This time, I was standing at a ticket booth in front of a structure built into a mountainside. I knew my ticket was prepaid for the event; I was just hoping I wasn't the star attraction.

A woman off to my left side spoke in a ridiculously matter-of-fact tone, as if nothing out of the ordinary was going on. "As soon as we check you through the gate, you can get

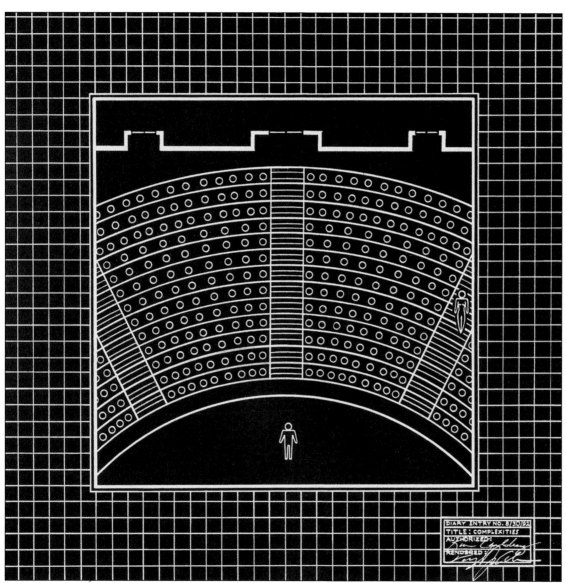

Complex-ities

acquainted with the complex." I stepped through the entrance and my consciousness collapsed again.

What a surprise! I woke up on a table! Naked! Don't these guys ever get tired of the same old job?

My body was propped on one side as three humanoid "doctors" leaned over me from the rear. Under happier circumstances, I might have been flattered by all the attention. A cold, metallic, square object was being pressed against my abdomen. My abdomen again? The thought was unbearable. Surrendering to the weight of my eyelids, I returned to dreamland, thankful for the drug that beckoned me.

Later on, I woke up in a lobby where many humans were milling around. They reminded me of patients waiting to endure their turns in the dentist's chair. With a start, I caught sight of two people across the room I recognized from BayWatch. *Running toward them, I stopped short as I came face to face with the last person I ever expected to see in these surrounding: Greg! Fearing it was my fault he was there, I choked on my own guilt and called out his name. "Oh my God, Greg, they got you, too!" He already had an angry scowl on his face and murmured, "Yeah," as he walked right past me without stopping. I hoped it was the aliens he was angry with and not me.*

I flashed on all the times I prayed to be able to prove abduction to anyone, especially Greg. I ached for him to know the truth but I never thought he'd find out this way. Then it hit me: by morning he wouldn't remember anything and for the first

time I was grateful for the aliens' parlor tricks with amnesia.

Time skipped a beat. I was sitting in a giant auditorium filled with thousands of people. A man, center stage, seemed to be answering questions. The moment I realized I could speak, I yelled out to him. "Why do you bring us here, allow us to be conscious part of the time, and still don't tell us what is going on?" *But he was too far away to hear me. I slumped into my seat, angry and frustrated.*

A young black woman, in casual military garb, glided up the aisle toward me and asked me to repeat my question, which I did.

She answered, "You are being prepared for something."

"Of course we're being prepared for something," *I said,* "but for what?"

"I can't tell you that."

"Then the least you can do is give me a hint." *I fumed, not trying to hide my sarcasm.*

A strange comment issued from behind me, and I turned around to see a fat lady with a smirk on her face. "Just tell her that when she does what she is being prepared to do, she will make a lot of money." *She was obviously trying to lighten the situation, but I thought she was as irritating as everything else in that house of detention.*

The black woman matched my sarcasm, parroting the fat lady with one deliberate difference: "If you ever make it to be doing what you are being prepared to do, you will probably

make a lot of money at it."

My class participation had not been appreciated and at that point the black woman escorted me from the auditorium. I was surprised she didn't ask me to carry my chair out into the hall as part of my reprimand.

When I stepped through the door, everything went black and when my eyes opened again, I recognized the neon numerals of my bedroom clock: 4:35 A.M. 👽

In the days that followed, I chose not to mention anything to Greg. It wasn't until many months later that I revealed I had seen him in the complex. As usual, he showed little interest. The aliens' enforced amnesia was working to curb his curiosity.

Later, while working at *BayWatch,* I approached the other two people I had seen during that abduction and struck up a conversation, inquiring about any unusual, "paranormal" events they might recall having experienced.

One of them drew a blank, but the other was curious as to my interest, so I tried to explain my reasons for asking without sounding like a candidate for a straight jacket.

A few sparks of recognition lit up his eyes as he listened and commented with relief, "That would explain some of the strange events of my childhood which I've always wondered about."

I suspect that the lethargy and selective memory loss which affects collections of humans in mass abductions may be the results of projected frequencies keyed to our brains, causing alterations in perception.

There have been times, as in the complex, when I move in and out of consciousness as I am led from room to room, as though it's all right to be aware in some locations, but not in others. Considering the amazing things I have seen, I would love to know what magnitude of secrets is so important that such extreme measures are required. I suppose I can grudgingly acknowledge that such a system of induced amnesia is an automatic guarantee of securing their clandestine activities.

With specific rooms tuned to a particular frequency, the flip of a switch could easily control the consciousness of hundreds, even thousands of people. This could be another reason for the many implants found in abductees' bodies and brains.

I don't know if I started paying more attention, or if there was an alien information boom in the media, but it seemed every time I turned on the television, which was infrequent, there was a program with an abduction theme, and on shows you wouldn't expect like *Quantum Leap*. The real kicker was when crew members of the Enterprise, on *Star Trek: The Next*

Generation, were taken in their sleep into another dimension and experimented on by ugly little creatures. Does life imitate art, or does art imitate life?

Fate arrived at my door, offering me my fifteen minutes of fame, and I accepted. I was approached by the media to tell my tale. I had seen the Friday night, prime time Fox Network program called *Sightings* and, compared to the way the subject of UFOs is normally reported, the program was relatively responsible. I decided, if my speaking out would help just one other person who was questioning his or her own sanity due to alien abductions, it would be worth it.

The time between the taping and the airing of the show was brief. There was hardly a chance for me to consider how going public was going to rattle what little remained intact of my life. Maybe that was a good thing.

A couple of days before "show time," I realized it was probably better to warn my friends at *BayWatch,* rather than deal with the astonished looks I would receive in the aftermath. I informed a few of my closest associates. Their disbelief was nothing compared to the jolt I was about to receive.

The still photographer on a production set is responsible for recording the action for publicity purposes. The ideal spot for the photographer is as close to the actual motion picture lens as he or she can get. It's good to be thin, which I am, because in order to get a good shot, you have to squeeze between the sound person, the camera operators, the director

of photography and last, but not least, the director.

Luckily, the crew of *BayWatch* was the greatest group with which one could ever hope to work, and I was forgiven more than once for being in the way or screwing things up. For some reason, even though I adore David Hasselhoff, I seemed to annoy him the most. I probably set the record in his career for blowing his takes with the sound of my shutter going off when I shouldn't have been shooting. Sorry David, I guess production stills aren't my forte. I don't know why he did it, but he always forgave me.

Sometimes it takes hours to set up shots that take only a few minutes to film. When the moment of actual shooting finally arrives, tension fills the air and everything is perfectly still in anticipation for the call, "Action!"

The scene we were about to shoot was on a cliff in Malibu overlooking the Pacific Ocean. David was to speed to a skidding stop in his lifeguard truck, jump out, and look over the cliff at whatever emergency was occurring below.

I was in a perfect position for the shot, inches to the right of the camera. The director called "Action!" The truck raced to the mark and kicked up a cloud of dust just feet from the lens. David, in full character, with heroic concern painted on his face, jumped out of the truck and looked directly into the lens. The next moment, he broke into a huge smile and shouted, "Kim, why don't you tell us all about your UFO encounters!"

I felt like someone had just dumped a bucket of ice water

over my head. I didn't know whether to kick him or to kiss him. With one sentence, the whole cast and crew knew. I guess I should have kissed him for getting it out of the way. David has a charming way of making people comfortable and making light of anything heavy, but I still slid under the camera and ran off the set.

Of course the director of *Sightings* used the most sensational cuts from my interview and when I saw the show, I knew I had really cut my throat. I was so nervous during the taping of the interview, I hadn't realized I actually spoke about the hybrid babies. Of course, that was the point highlighted most, to the extent a "re-creation" of a fetus in a bottle was inserted into the program.

If I hadn't been an independent contractor who gets paid by the day, I would have called in sick the following Monday morning. On the way to work, I fantasized that maybe there had been a blackout throughout the rest of Los Angeles Friday night and no one else saw the show.

When I got to the beach, I was as quiet as I could be, hoping to go unnoticed. I was noticed, but in a very different way than I expected. The members of the crew would casually come up to me and mention they saw the show, like it was no big deal. Then they would tell me their own UFO stories.

I heard more personal UFO stories than I had ever heard in one day, including in my support group meetings.

A person I had been very close to for years came up to me and said, "I know exactly what you are talking about," as he proceeded to tell me his own abduction experiences. I was pleasantly shocked. It was beginning to look like this was a common occurrence no one was talking about until I opened my mouth. How could so many people be silent about such an incredible thing?

Regardless of the corroboration I received, it wasn't real for Greg. I can only imagine what he must have gone through back then and the kind of comments he had to put up with. Whatever he had to contend with, I never heard about it. He tried to make light of the whole issue, but abduction silently eroded what remained of our relationship.

The next week, we were shooting a boat explosion scene off the coast at Paradise Cove. Quite often, I am required to shoot only the most exciting scenes, so if a routine scene is being shot in the morning, I get a break. That particular morning was one of those cases, and, by the time I got to the set, the cast and crew had already been offshore on the cruiser for several hours. In the meantime, the tide had picked up and the waves were making it impossible for the inflatable transfer craft to get back to shore. I was stranded on the beach without much of a chance of getting to the cruiser, but I didn't dare leave or I would have lost a day's pay.

Foggy days at the beach are very romantic, and that day the fog was so thick you could cut it. I sat in the sand enjoying the mood, when a gorgeous man in dark sunglasses screeched into the parking lot in a shiny new Corvette. Probably a guest star; who else would be wearing sunglasses in the fog?

I was sure he was just another egomaniac who would only be around for one episode, so I decided I'd have a little fun with him.

"Mr. Guest Star" strutted up to the pier and asked, "Is this the place?"

"Yeah, but the inflatable can't make it in to shore, so we're stuck here...and by the way, did you see me on *Sightings* Friday night talking about my alien abductions?"

I'd never seen anyone react the way he did. He came two inches from my face, slowly lowered his glasses and said in a severe tone, "Do you actually see them when they come? I never see them when they come for me, I only feel their presence. I'd give anything to see them!"

He was being dead honest. I stared at him dumfounded. The joke was on me!

We spent the day strolling the beach, discussing our individual theories, and became good friends.

I have several recurring "dreams" about massive fleets of UFOs and the following vision is the one I have most often. I don't know what it means, but I hope it doesn't portend an actual future invasion.

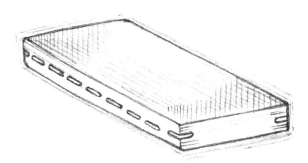

INVASION
September 2, 1992

Dear Diary:

f I've had this "dream" once, I've had it a hundred times: With each wave, the stinging salt water flayed my naked skin as I stood shivering in the icy ocean of an unfamiliar, uninhabited coastline.

As though black thunderclouds rode in on the wind, the expanse before me was suddenly overshadowed by a thousand shimmering disks. This aerial display of regal beauty was defiled by an ominous aura of malevolence emitting from the invading armada.

These dark gods were the new masters of the Earth, and I was overwhelmed with terror!

Not only were UFOs in my nights and on television, they showed up at work! A photographer doesn't have a lot of homework as do other people who work in production. I don't have scripts to read or shot lists to make. I don't even have to know what the episodes are about. All I have to do is show up when I'm supposed to and take good pictures. With the way my life was going, about all I could manage to do was show up. Of course, with my insomnia, early calls were exceedingly difficult.

Invasion

IN YOUR HONOR
1992, Date Not Recorded

Dear Diary:

This morning, I groggily made my way to Lifeguard Headquarters where I was told we were shooting a new episode today. When I walked out onto the beach, what I saw was so eerie I dropped my camera bags in disbelief.

The beach was lined with huge radio-receiving disks and dozens of extras were walking around wearing caps that said "UFO." If it was a joke, it was a pretty expensive one. I immediately ran over to Doug, who was directing, and asked, "What in the world is going on here?" Doug responded, "You mean, you don't know?"

"Know what?"

"I don't believe it…are you serious? This episode was written in your honor and no one told you? I even have a scene I want you to be in!"

I burst out laughing! It was so surreal. My outrageous, unbelievable life circumstance was right before me in a Hollywood production. I looked up to the sky and shouted, "Are you guys getting all of this?"

Opposite page: The "gang" at *BayWatch*. I'm third from the left.

In Your Honor

I have met people in the UFO and metaphysical circles who object to the term "abductee." These people choose more neutral substitutions, such as "contactee," or the newest term, "experiencer," to avoid a negative connotation.

It seems people of contact, who refer to their experiences as abductions, are looked down upon as being victim personalities. *I* am not a victim personality. If anything, I am the opposite: I am positive, productive, and happy. Even with years of abduction, I glean everything I can from these unwanted experiences.

So I believe it is time to set the record straight, and call a spade a spade. These are my definitions of "Contact" versus "Abduction." You decide.

CONTACT

1. A knock on the door, a phone call, or a written invitation.

2. Verbal or telepathic communication.

3. Accepting and agreeing upon contact; when and where.

4. Meeting while fully conscious.

5. Being free to move on your own volition.

6. Sitting or standing comfortably while conversing.

7. Enjoying a mutual exchange.

8. "Let's do this again sometime."

ABDUCTION

1. Intrusion into your home; being snuck up on in the middle of the night.

2. No communication or explanation from your abductors, only silence.

3. Resisting your abductors.

4. Rendered unconscious with drugs and other types of mind manipulations.

5. Physically incapacitated and dragged out of your bed against your will.

6. Strapped to a table while physical experiments are performed on your body.

7. Psychological and emotional experiments performed on your mind.

I am not an overly emotional woman. As a matter of fact, I have been accused of being less emotional than the average person. Maybe something has rubbed off on me from the extraterrestrial company I keep.

The first time I saw the likeness of a Grey alien in my own reality was in the restaurant of the Los Angeles Airport Hilton during a convention. The restaurant was packed and I was having lunch with a group of friends, one of whom, Keith, asked if I would like to see his art. I excitedly accepted. He pulled a box, approximately two feet square, from the booth seat and put it in the middle of the table. When he proudly unveiled his master-piece, I burst into uncontrollable tears. The art was a marble sculpture of a Zeta.

Never before, or since, have I reacted so irrationally to an inanimate object. That was the first hint that the suppressed abduction memories I was harboring must have been horrendous.

Metaphysicians believe you manifest your own reality, and so do I. They will say, "On a soul level you are creating these events to learn lessons." Of course, but that does not negate how painful they are on a physical level.

We are all spiritual beings in physical form. We are all here to gain knowledge. The starving children in Africa, on a soul level, are learning something, but that doesn't mean we shouldn't be compassionate.

"Contactees" or "experiencers" or whatever you want to call them, have suffered extreme manipulation that traumatically

impacts their bodies and minds—and they deserve help. It doesn't make them anymore "victim" personalities than someone who falls on broken glass and needs stitches.

Unfortunately, at this time, there are relatively few places abductees can get medical or psychiatric treatment. When we seek assistance, abductees are misdiagnosed and treated for hallucinations or some other "familiar" psychosis. Of course, this compounds the problem. The following is my personal experience of turning to the "psychiatric community" for help.

I was born into a middle-class family, one of three children. At the age of fourteen I made some very hard decisions after one of the most shattering occurrences in my life: my father's death. Unfortunately all my mother inherited was sole responsibility as breadwinner. My mother's life was terrible, and I vowed I would never be burdened the same way. Education would be my ticket, but I came hazardously close to losing that opportunity.

During my sophomore year of college, while working my way through school as a model, I was forced to see a psychologist for a phobia that appeared out of the blue one day and ended up altering the course of my life.

My major was fine art, but I was becoming increasingly excited about the magic of photography. During my modeling

career, I saw many photographs of myself and I was always surprised at how every photographer could make me so much better looking in pictures than I was in real life. I decided to take some photography courses myself to understand the transformational secrets of film.

One of my photo instructors convinced a selection of the best photographers in the business to speak to his classes for special, extra credit seminars. He put together quite a lineup of talent. Unfortunately, the lectures were held on Saturdays and I worked weekends.

But there was one photographer I was determined not to miss: Harry Langdon. I was a great admirer of his style and if I had to play hooky from work, it would be worth it.

On the morning of the scheduled lecture, I went into an outrageous fantasy while getting dressed. What if Harry Langdon did more than speak? What if he actually decided to put on a demonstration and chose me to be his subject? I would have photos by Harry Langdon in my portfolio! I had such an imagination back then. Nevertheless, I arrived at the studio wearing my best attire in hopes of inspiring a modeling session.

Mr. Langdon's Beverly Hills "palace" was really something! The lobby was a gallery of his most famous celebrity portraits. He was truly a master and a humbling influence for any aspiring artist.

After a few hours of listening to Mr. Langdon speak on

success, I had an even greater respect for the man. He started his business in a garage, and went on to build his studio with the aid of a bank loan he secured with nothing more than his portfolio as collateral. Now that's impressive!

Just when I thought the session was about to end, I heard a voice call out, "Now I would like to demonstrate some of the techniques I have discussed, and I would like the little girl in white to be my model." As I glanced around the room I noticed all eyes were staring in my direction...I was the one wearing white. We moved into the shooting area of the studio, which was an enormous, pristine, white cove with a platform in the middle. Shooting areas are commonly white and curved to eliminate shadows. The area glowed. The white walls and rounded edges of the room reflected the light with perfect consistency. The space was soft and shadowless.

Harry asked me to come up on the stage and gestured to his assistants to start setting up equipment. From the elevated stage, I looked into the eyes of my peers and suddenly my joy turned to panic.

My body reacted as if death had just walked into the room. My mouth became parched, my heart pounded, I was perspiring, and everything went out of focus. The next thing I knew, someone was holding a cold rag to my forehead and a glass of water to my lips. I felt Harry's hand on my shoulder and heard him say, "I'm sorry." I told him he had nothing to be sorry for and that I was all right, but I was lying. I had no idea what had caused the panic

attack. I had never experienced anything like that before. I went home and didn't leave my house for a week.

The embarrassment of collapsing in front of my classmates was bad, but nothing I couldn't overcome. That wasn't the problem. Something deeper and darker had been touched and was begging for release, but my mind rejected the secret that was desperately trying to claw its way to the surface. I sank into depression and isolated myself from everyone.

After missing school for a week, I realized everything I had been striving for would evaporate if I didn't pull it together. The next day I made myself go back to class. It was like walking through hell. Every time eyes fell upon me, my body would react the way it did in Harry Langdon's studio...it would panic.

By the time I arrived at class I was shaking like a leaf. I slinked into the room praying to go unseen, but the instructor, trying to be kind, made sure that wasn't going to happen. "Hello, Kim, it's good to have you back," he announced. I nodded in acknowledgment and raced to a seat in the back of the room to escape the curious looks. At the end of the hour, I realized I hadn't heard a word, I had been too preoccupied with the terror of being noticed.

Being looked at was suddenly so agonizing I avoided the public completely. I stopped modeling, never got in front of a camera again, and dropped out of school. I was broke in more ways than one, but somehow I had enough sense to find help through a state program where they referred me to a therapist.

After months of treatment, my therapist confessed, "Kim, I can't help you, I give up. I have no clue what is causing this phobia, and I am not helping you alleviate it. I could keep you on as a client, but it wouldn't be right."

I was devastated! I spent the rest of that day at the beach, crying my heart out. I had worked so hard to build a better life for myself than that of my mother's, and some cruel twist of fate had put this unexplainable mental/emotional anguish into what should have been the best years of my life. Fortunately, I didn't have the courage to end it all. I accepted I would just have to continue with my incurable disability.

Luckily, I still had my love for art and my cameras. The next semester I returned to school a very different kind of person and would not find a cure for my phobia for almost fifteen years.

STAGE FRIGHT
Regression

Dear Diary:

I've had my mind blown before, but this regression really took the cake. Not until fifteen minutes after it was over did I realize the formidable impact this event had on my life. This is what I recalled: A black fog lifted from my mind. My inert naked body was splayed like a rag doll across a low, metal table. My head and one arm dangled haphazardly over the hard edge. The shadowless, crescent room glowed white, but no light source was visible.

I could see my image in a large screen or mirror suspended at an angle overhead. I drooled from lifeless lips, too dulled by drugs to salvage even a shred of dignity.

The table was positioned on a stage and, when my head rolled to one side, I looked downward over my audience. My stare was reflected a hundred times from a sea of pitiless black eyes which filled the hall. A presence standing behind me, who I could not see, began performing some sort of demonstration upon my body with the clinical attitude typically reserved for cadavers. I was the main subject of a medical lecture! Treated like an inanimate slab of human flesh and served up to feed the aliens' insatiable curiosity. 👽

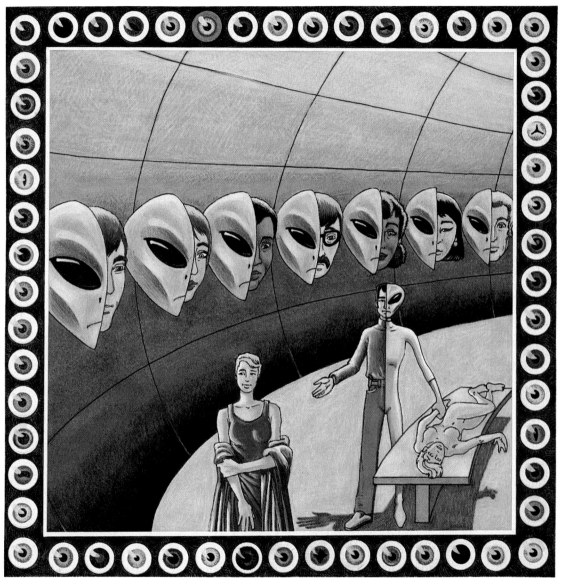

Stage Fright

The panoply of medical methods used by the Greys rivals the wildest of our emergency-room procedures. In addition to the insensitive and irritating insertion of tubes and probes into every imaginable orifice, the aliens have no compunction about flaying our bodies like lab rats: they open our skulls and chests, and prod our internal organs with the slapdash attitude of surgeons on speed.

Fortunately, their advanced knowledge also permits them to reassemble our flesh-puppet frames with little sign of their invasive intrusions. A few fine red traces are all that remain to mark the unsolicited examinations.

After the regression, my mind paced back fifteen years to Harry Langdon's studio. The coved shooting space with the elevated platform had been the exact duplication of the interior of the alien surgical theater, where I had also been "the center of attention," triggering, in my subconscious, the memory of that devastating abduction.

After years of living with my disability, I had become so used to it and had adjusted my life around it so precisely that it was almost unnoticeable. I successfully completed four more years of college without ever giving a speech to a class. I persuaded my teachers to excuse me from such dreaded duty with the aid of a note from my therapist.

The months following the regression, the remainder of my mysterious phobia dissipated, and I was healed by realizing the initial source of my problem. I am now back in front of the

camera, constantly being interviewed on television. I speak about the uncomfortable subject of abduction with only slight nervousness. What a shame I had to suffer all those years because too little is known about the phenomenon of alien abduction.

It was sadly obvious why I didn't want to be looked at. Being the guinea pig to a room full of cold-blooded alien biologists was grounds enough, but there was more.

The aliens perform "mind scans" by getting as close as they can get to their victim's face and using their will to take over. Nothing can be hidden from them; it is a form of mental rape.

The Greys use the same staring technique for sedating, paralyzing, or inserting fantasies for the sake of their research.

"PREYING" MANTIS
Regression

Dear Diary:

'm tied down—restrained at both wrists and ankles as if I was criminally insane. I rail against the drugs pounding through my veins. They are wise to keep me bound. I'd lash out and gouge their hideous eyes from their sockets if given half the chance.

"It" arrives. It's a ghastly creature, a walking stick topped by a bulbous head with gargantuan, glistening eyes. The sickest imagination couldn't conjure up this vermin wraith. My mind rebels, even as it is forced to accept the certainty of the monster's vile presence.

It approaches on spidery legs and hovers over my naked body like a vulture too eager to wait for death. I turn my head away, refusing to give it the satisfaction of acknowledgment, but it presses so close I feel my breath sucked up for its own.

It hungers for my mind—it must devour my every thought, my every emotion as if these are its sustenance. It's a voyeur, a parasite...a vampire that drains me of my will.

It mocks me—toys with me—wallowing in its omnipotence. I can feel its dark pleasure knowing I must eventually succumb, as always, to its indomitable mental power. I am jailed in a purgatory of anticipation before it moves in for the "kill."

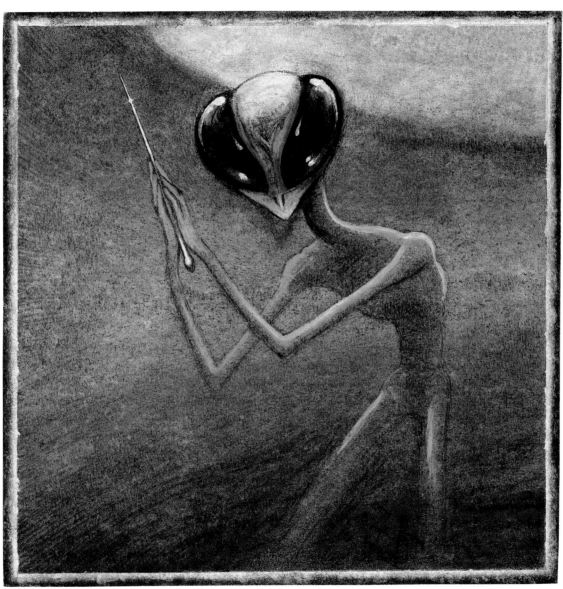

Mantis

My barriers break down; weakened, I can no longer resist. Its eyes thrust forward—a papery, wrinkled forehead presses against mine. Its skeletal frame shivers in victory while it "swallows" my mind whole!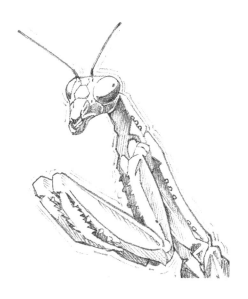

I sensed the "mantis" was the one that held the highest level of authority among the Greys: the "queen bee." This would tend to reinforce my perception that the small "workers," the larger "doctors," the hybrid "nurses," and the loathsome mantis are direct parallels to an insect social structure, which may explain the unique nature of the mantis in comparison to the monotonous physical uniformity of each individual within the lower "castes."

**J. ALLEN HYNEK
CENTER FOR
UFO STUDIES**

UFO Resource Facility
Library and Publication Sales

2457 W. Peterson Ave.
Chicago, IL 60659
(312) 271-3611

October 10, 1992

Kim Carlsberg
P.O. Box 1154
Pacific Palisades, CA   90272

Dear Kim:

I've finished reviewing the results of the questionnaires you completed. Sorry it's taken awhile to get back to you,
but I was tied up with the start of the fall term at the university.

Your MMPI results indicate that your personality falls into a normal range on what are called the "primary" scales.
These measure such things as paranoia, schizoid behavior, hysteria, introversion, and so forth. If anything, the results
indicate that you are moderately outgoing and extroverted. You also do not manifest any overt symptoms of anxiety
about your life and seem to have a strong sense of self. The MMPI did pick up some complaints you have about your
health, but we've already talked about these on the phone.

The results from the ICMI indicate that you have a healthy fantasy life and enjoy imagination and creativity, but
not to excess. You also have had many unusual experiences, such as precognition, out-of-body experiences, seeing
spirits, and so forth, which means you are open to such things and don't have a rigid worldview.

All in all, you seem to be well-adjusted, as measured by these few questionnaires. Obviously you are still integrating
the experiences you have had into your life, so you may not feel perfectly whole, but there is no reason why you
shouldn't be able to reach that goal.

I hope you find this information useful.

Sincerely,

Mark Rodeghier

I finally received the results of the psychological tests which CUFOS
asked me to take. Thank goodness they believe I'm sane!

Thanksgiving weekend, my friend Diane (whom I met in an abductee support meeting) and I went with the Sierra Club's photographers' group to China Lake Naval Base. Our mission was to look for evidence of an underground base behind the pretense of taking pictures of the ancient petroglyphs that adorn the cliff faces nearby.

Steve, the owner of the photo lab I use, had put together about twenty-five shooters for the three-day camping trip. As synchronicity would have it, I happen to be at the lab when Steve got a call from one of the photographers who had to cancel at the last minute.

When Steve explained there was a year-long waiting list to get on the base, it cinched my decision to offer myself as a replacement. It was also a perfect opportunity to test my new five-degree sleeping bag.

In our enthusiasm, Diane and I committed the cardinal sin of camping. We packed everything but the kitchen sink and were burdened the entire weekend. And, of course, I took too many cameras.

We spent the first night camping in the beauty of Red Rock Canyon National Park in the Mojave Desert. Unfortunately, we got there after dark and couldn't see the canyon.

It was so cold I considered sleeping in the back of the truck

instead of in my two-person tent, but that idea died quickly when I went to pull out our supplies. The ten-gallon plastic water container had been crushed by things shifting around. The carpeting on the floor of the truck was soaked, and so was the firewood.

Luckily we camped next to a "dad," his teenage sons, and their friends. These guys were the greatest. They unloaded the truck, brought us dry firewood, built the fire, and became our new best friends.

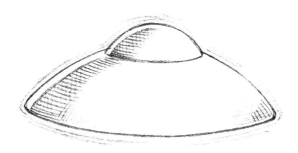

CHINA LAKE SYNDROME
November 22, 1992

Dear Diary:

My five-degree bag passed the test. I was cozy the entire night; that is, if in fact I was in the bag! I went to sleep, but when I opened my eyes I was standing erect, marveling at the Tolkienesque quality of the strange new world around me. The colors and forms could have only come from my imagination. But I was unquestionably awake and not imagining them.

From what I could make of it, I was positioned in the center of a courtyard outlined by monolithic rocks. I couldn't tell if the formations were natural or elegantly carved facades. With their graceful lines and curves, they were more reminiscent of mythological animals than functional structures.

There were passageways at every corner: open floodgates for the unearthly, warm hue that washed over the land from a distant, unobscured horizon.

Reinforcing the fairy-tale feel, a great shadow cast over the courtyard, as if the foot of Goliath stepped down from heaven, ready to squash me like an ant. I looked up, but instead of a foot, the belly of an immense mothership came to rest on top of the rock formations, using them as landing pads. The ship was the size of a small city!

China Lake

At this point I realized I wasn't alone. There were several humans to my right who looked as perplexed as I felt. White light rained down upon our heads as a smaller craft dislodged from the underside of the mothership. I wouldn't have known it was there if it hadn't separated; it was masterfully camouflaged.

Unfortunately, my spellbinding storytellers, whoever they were, decided I'd had enough for one night and abruptly closed the book. I was back in my tent lying on my side, and leaning on one elbow with my head propped against my hand, as though still waiting for the end of the story.

I checked on Diane; she was sound asleep. I lay there and stared at the seam in the top of the tent, wondering if she had been somewhere in the group of people in the courtyard with me, if she had been "zapped" unconscious and I was abducted alone, or if I should stop eating spicy food before going to bed at night.

When I woke up (again) the next morning, I knew by the intensity of the light and temperature in the tent that I had over-slept. I could hear Diane scuffling around outside so I unzipped the flap to find a cup of coffee being shoved in my face. Diane joked, "I was wondering if you were ever going to wake up."

"Diane, I had the most amazing dream last night! It was about a spaceship!"

Her mouth dropped, "Oh, my God, so did I!"

"Don't tell me, just get a couple of pens and some paper. I'll stay here; you go to the other side of the camp and draw exactly

what you remember."

    We spent five minutes sketching, pulled the beach chairs up to the fire, and exchanged drawings and looks of disbelief. Our sketches were of the identical scout craft from different perspectives. My point of view was from directly beneath it. Diane's was from the side which allowed her to see the top of the craft. I call that confirmation! ☻

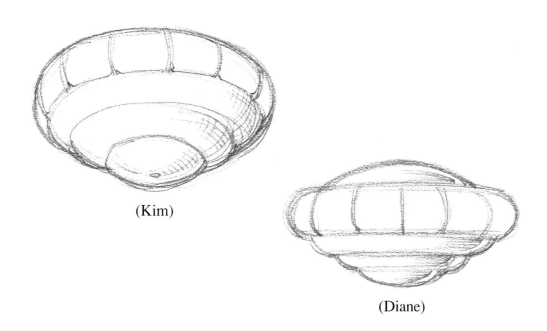

(Kim)

(Diane)

Artist's rendering of original drawings.

Many scientists do not accept the possibility that UFOs could be intelligently controlled spacecraft from other worlds because the vast distances between star systems would require years, if not lifetimes, to traverse, even at the speed of light.

However, recent theories on the nature of space/time propose methods of travel which circumvent the lightspeed limitation. Robert Lazar, for example, a physicist who has recently come forward and publicly admitted he was hired to study the alien disks retrieved by the military, has confirmed the craft employ a sophisticated drive system which bends the space/time continuum.

This has the effect, he says, of warping the fabric of space, permitting the ship to "pull" the destination to its location, until they overlap. The craft then anchors itself to the gravity of the destination and allows that destination to "snap back" to its previous position. The craft then rides the wave as *part of the destination* instead of simply traveling in a linear fashion "on top" of it like the conventional spacecraft we currently use here on Earth.

Therefore, the distance from one star to another is negated and the journey is instantaneous.

With this kind of technology at their disposal, the aliens come and go as they please with less thought than we give when taking an airplane trip to a nearby city.

I had the pleasure of spending the Christmas holidays with my friend Joanie at her beautiful adobe-style estate, situated ten minutes from Santa Fe, New Mexico, in the quaint little village of Tesuque.

It was my first visit to New Mexico and I was astonished at the natural beauty of the land. The red clay bluffs, lush vegetation, and crystal blue skies layered with puffy clouds created an artist's paradise. I instantly knew why Ansel Adams was inspired to take some of his most famous photographs there. I have never burned as much film as I did visiting that "Land of Enchantment."

Just being on this land was a religious experience, so it was easy to understand why the Native Americans who live there are such spiritual people. Their respect for the inner world is reflected everywhere in their lives, but most notably through their ritual art and such artifacts as sand paintings, kachinas, and dreamcatchers.

But the Southwest is also known for another kind of otherworldly observation: UFO sightings, beginning with the famous UFO crash in Roswell, New Mexico, in 1947.

I was a little nervous to be in that activity vortex, with my own tendency for attracting visitors, but I tried to put it out of my mind and get on with the business at hand: enjoying my Christmas vacation.

Joanie had prepared the guest wing—a large bedroom with a fireplace and floor-to-ceiling windows overlooking acres of

virgin landscape. I left the blinds open when I went to bed so I could appreciate the starlight glistening on the snow—a rare sight for a Southern California gal. Seldom have I experienced that kind of quiet.

I felt like royalty in the antique, wrought-iron bed that was fitted with an overstuffed mattress and lightly starched linens. I actually fell asleep quite easily for once, but I didn't sleep long.

SEASON'S GREETINGS
December, 1992

Dear Diary:

I woke up in the middle of the night to see the world lit up like I was on the inside of a red electric Christmas tree bulb. I heard a loud buzzing and a thought went through my head, "That refrigerator sure is loud tonight." *(Even though the kitchen was halfway across the main house.) But for some strange reason that explanation satisfied me and I immediately passed out.*

I woke up again in what seemed only a few minutes, lying on my side with my back parallel to the edge of the bed. Instantly, fear triggered my adrenaline. Something was literally breathing down my back. I thought my heart would burst through my chest before I had a chance to talk myself down. "Okay, Kim, you've been through this enough times to know you always live through it. It's going to be all right. Now just turn over verrry *slowly and when you are ready, open your eyes." I kept my eyes tightly closed and moved methodically in increments of an inch at a time. I'm sure I didn't breathe for several minutes. When I was flat on my back, I popped my eyes open and a thought went through my head that was so bizarre, I burst out laughing! The telepathically implanted words were, "Gee, I love waking up and finding you here!"*

A little pointed chin was two inches from my nose. I was so mesmerized by humor coming from a Grey, my fear vanished. That was absolutely the last thing I ever thought would happen at the sight of a Grey by my bedside. It was such a hysterically absurd statement, I had to reconsider my conclusions about these beings. They didn't go out of character often, but when they did, they really went over the top.

I studied the alien chin with fascination. It was so pointed I imagined it would hurt to touch it. A moment later, I was unconscious again.

I awoke a third time, standing in the corner of the room as I observed two Greys pointing a sharp metal object at the tailbone of someone lying in the bed where I had been. Oddly enough, that person looked suspiciously like me. 👽

More of my experiences started happening outside of the usual examination chambers. That was a breath of fresh air!

Season's Greetings

TRIAD
February 2, 1993

Dear Diary:

I had a "dream" that I was alone, standing beneath three triangular spacecraft. One jetted forward and put on a performance I knew was just for me. It propelled a white material out into the space in front of it. The parachute-like fabric fluttered in the wind and then cocooned itself around the ship, camouflaging it like a cloud. The second craft advanced and did the same thing. The third followed suit. They were showing me how they cloaked themselves.

The next thing I knew I was in a very strange place. My first thought was extremely disturbing...I was standing on what I thought was another planet. The lighting was eerie: an orange glow surrounded everything, but I could not find its source. The landscape was as barren as a dried-up river bed. My next thought was even more alarming...I knew I had been there before!

Directly in front of me was a simple adobe-like structure with no glass in the windows and no door; just an opening. I looked around in all directions. Off in the distance, a group of Greys were headed my way. Coming up behind me was a small gathering of humanoid figures in elegant flight suits. Directly to my left was an ordinary human couple.

Triad

Panic set in. I knew it was useless to try and hide from the Greys, but the fight-or-flight instinct had already kicked in. I raced toward the adobe building followed by the couple. The shelter was empty but there was an opening to a cellar, so we jumped into the hole and curled up on the cellar floor. No words were exchanged between the two other people and myself as we huddled together in anguished anticipation.

My mind went blank, then revived to see one of the humanoid aviators, a male, standing a few feet in front of me. I quickly took inventory of my situation. I was now standing outside of the adobe house. The couple were nowhere to be found; neither were the Greys.

A flood of telepathic information filled my mind. I knew the man before me had been one of the pilots of the triangular craft. As I took in every detail of his physical image, I realized I was connected to him in some way. A strong spiritual link was becoming apparent, but it was indefinable.

He was a young, handsome, Caucasian male with beaming blue-green eyes. He stood about 5' 10" tall and had long, wavy, light-brown hair. As we stood silently sizing each other up, two more figures approached, also wearing flight suits.

I heard a rumble, and out of the corner of my left eye I saw a huge steam roller barreling in our direction. Without saying a word, the three "pilots" walked toward the moving machine and lay down in front of it. Their bodies disappeared under the giant roller. I was horrified, but instantly a voice in my head

comforted me. "This is to show you the body is only a shell." The tank moved on and I ran over to the crushed carcasses. All that remained were splinters of hard plastic. I picked one up and it dissolved in my hand.

I awakened from the "dream." It was 2:45 A.M. I don't know who or what the humanoid beings were, but the experience was a welcome change from all the other encounters which involved the Greys. Whoever they were, I hope to see them again sometime.

deepening

SECOND CHANCES
1993, Date Not Recorded

Dear Diary:

My tranquil repose was abruptly terminated by an unexpected tour of a celestial tailor shop. I rubbed the sleep from my eyes, then attempted to bring my surroundings into focus: everything was soft-edged and diffused, as though formed from clouds.

A puzzling sight stretched out before me as rows upon rows of gossamer beings of light operated what appeared to be sewing machines. They were intent on their task, though what manner of garment such spirits would wear, I had no clue. The entities were so busy in their serious concern and dedication to their work, I wasn't even noticed.

As I continued on, I became aware of someone directing me by thought from behind. I was not allowed to turn around to face my transcendental tour guide, but was forced to pay strict attention to the gravity of my situation. I felt suspended between heaven and hell as I was fed the vital statistics of "the Station," this realm I now walked through where people go when they die too soon!

The purpose of the Station was illustrated as we came upon two human beings, a man and a woman, who clearly stood out in solid relief against the two radiant, ethereal souls hovering

Second Chances

before them.

I was suddenly overcome with pity for the fragile, fear-struck humans as they received the tragic news of their predicament: they had died prematurely and would have to be returned to Earth to be reinserted back into their lives at some point before their deaths had occurred. They could then fulfill their destinies.

I was mesmerized by the skill and compassion with which the beings of light delicately, but sternly, handled the bewildered couple. It was obvious the entities held a position of authority close to that of angelic. It's a shame this couple's first face-to-face encounter with an angel had to come under such awkward circumstances.

Not wanting to stick my nose in other people's business, I started to back away when my invisible usher made it quite clear it was his plan to place me close enough to hear every last word and still remain unnoticed. At this point my guide informed me the humans would never know anything unusual had happened to them once they were back in their bodies. The memory of their demise and their visit to the Station would be erased. I was so taken by the exchange, it never dawned on me...I was next in line. ☻

When I was returned to my bed, I woke up high from the experience. I realized the Station is a very real place, though the sewing machines were only my mind's interpretation of the kind of work that is done there: mending errors so no one ever knows mistakes have been made. More than seamstresses, the beings are spiritual surgeons, sewing up holes in the fabric of souls.

The creation of a new species is much more complicated than merely mixing DNA, especially when it involves humans. Our emotions are difficult enough for *us* to understand, so the Greys, who seem to lack emotion, are extremely curious about such matters as love, sex, fear, and the basic desire to survive.

In my encounters with Greys, I am almost always studied on one of these four aspects. The aliens have the ability to re-create scenarios that are absolutely lifelike. I don't know how they accomplish this, but the closest comparisons I can make would be a holographic projection, a mentally induced "virtual reality," or a combination of the two. Sometimes they simply show up in our reality disguised as humans and act out their scripts. Whatever their methods, the settings they concoct to explore our makeup are as convincing as any real situation, and a person has no choice but to react to the circumstances invoked by the aliens.

THE FEAR FACTOR
1993, Date Not Recorded

Dear Diary:

A *s I prepared for bed, my inner voice cautioned me to be wary of this night, so it was with trepidation that I coaxed myself to sleep. Sure enough, my rest was assaulted by five disturbing "dreams." This was the most horrifying one: I physically materialized along with four other sorry subjects into a manufactured psychodrama.*

Moon rays glared off the jagged edges of serrated steel debris flung throughout a forgotten junkyard. Damp piles of discarded personal possessions were heaped about like cast-off snake skins. Mounds of decaying man-made objects protruded like the tombstones of a disposable age.

Our group, placed here by some Machiavellian chess master, nervously moved without a word through the dark labyrinth of yesterday's self-indulgence. My bare feet sank into a foul sludge of rodent droppings as I fought against the lure of an undivulged pied piper. Held hostage by this irresistible force, we were dragged to the feet of an apparition: a crucified gargoyle of rotting flesh.

Fueled by our fear, the lifeless carcass resurrected and in one desperate leap, tore itself from its unholy shrine. The animated corpse pursued us and we scattered like frightened

Fear Factor

rabbits as blood sprayed in all directions from its ruptured wounds.

As the theatrics played out, they all smacked of a grade "B" monster movie and the fingerprints of the Grey puppetmaster began to show through the smoke and mirrors of this stygian trial.

The absurdity of the scene became more pronounced and I burst out laughing, blowing away the weak mental mortar of their preposterous projection.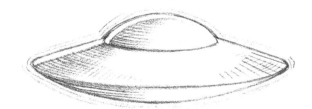

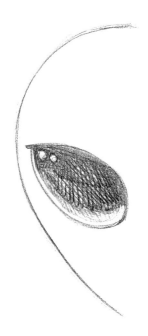

Beyond My Wildest Dreams

PSYCHIC SEDUCTION
March 14, 1993

Dear Diary:

I don't remember going to bed last night. This is what I do remember: I was suddenly running a desperately urgent errand, although I had no idea what it was. My entire driveway was shrouded in a mysterious fog as I reached for the door handle of my Toyota 4-Runner. I don't even remember how I got outside. It felt like I was plucked from my life and dropped into someone's already-running virtual reality game.

I envisioned my circumstance was the result of some child deity with a short attention span: a demigod whose most frivolous thoughts effortlessly give birth to universes of which it is hardly aware. Meanwhile, the spontaneous creations, such as myself, are doomed to act out this lord's unconscious fantasies long after it has forgotten them.

A bright, diffused light from somewhere above the fog was suddenly eclipsed by an enormous, wing-shaped craft that shadowed the whole block. I slipped into the truck, hoping the descending presence would overlook such small prey as me, but I knew I wasn't going to be so lucky.

I was so frightened I forgot I could lock the doors with the push of a single button, even though door locks would have posed no obstacle to the force which closed in around me.

Seduction

I prayed to become invisible before this mechanical scavenger captured me with its talons of electric blue light. My mind was suddenly saturated with visions of being eaten alive, or worse, becoming like one of the butterflies in a bug collection: my arms and legs stretched wide, and my torso impaled with a giant straight pin, while spending eternity affixed to the black velvet in the treasure chest of an adolescent alien.

I tensed at a loud rapping on the back window. The truck rocked and shook as a brilliant shaft of light invaded the interior. Since disappearing was not an option, I decided to face the fear and hold on to what remained of my personal power. As I turned around in my seat, a pulsating beam of energy shot into my forehead and surrounded my entire body. As I had feared, the vibrations consumed me.

In the next nonsequitur moment, a man jumped into the front seat beside me. The fact that he had appeared out of nowhere was not half as disquieting as who he was! It was my ex-husband's best friend, Mark, whom I hadn't seen in ten years! Before I could say a word, he looked into my eyes and I felt a familiar psychic manipulation begin. He was trying to seduce me, but I didn't fall for it. It may have looked like Mark physically, but I knew that alien essence all too well.

I refused to make eye contact and didn't say a word. He (or it) realized the ploy was failing, and clumsily apologized for trying to convince me to have sex with him. I pretended to accept, thinking that was the simplest way out of the situation.

This time, the aliens accepted defeat and the next moment I was in my bed. It was 2:14 A.M. Wow, an apology from the Greys! Now that's what I call progress! 👽

The man in this story and I were never physically attracted to one another, so this experience reinforces my theory that the aliens have no understanding of human sexuality, and the fact I haven't seen or heard from him in over ten years proves they haven't got a clue about relationships.

I have been taken to places I can describe in no other way than "alien environments." Other locations seemed to be man-made structures. The belief is, one day our government made a Faustian pact: alien technology in exchange for breeding rights. It is no secret this country has many underground facilities. Numerous military personnel have confessed to seeing alien craft as well as aliens in some of these bases.

I have a feeling our government knows many of the tricks the aliens use as far as mind control, and probably a variety of other nasty secrets.

But why does everyone have to pick on me?

SISTERS OF SACRIFICE
1993, Date Not Recorded

Dear Diary:

*S*leep broke its embrace. The claustrophobic interior of a small, damp cellar imprisoned me. A narrow rectangle of light near the low ceiling was the only window in the room and, stretching on tiptoes, I peered between rusted bars.

My eyes, at ground level, witnessed a maelstrom of commotion. An asphalt tarmac extended in all directions. Military personnel scurried around grounded aircraft, performing routine maintenance checks.

As my mind grappled with the disturbing recognition I was on an airbase, three flying saucers moved into view and hovered as if they were waiting for a signal to land. My blood ran cold! The implication that the aliens and the military were cohorts struck like a bullet to my brain and filled me with absolute dread.

Up until then, my biggest fear was of alien abduction, but in that moment a new and more monumental fear was born. It was evident by the military personnel's nonchalant reaction to the disks that something enormously deceitful and corrupt was occurring.

My body collapsed in disbelief. Abduction had destroyed my trust in God. Now, my belief in my own country was decimated

Sisters of Sacrifice

by this apparent betrayal. Was the military delivering me into the hands of the enemy?

The hard-soled shoes of a pack of CIA goons marched past the window, kicking up a cloud of dust and obscuring my view. The door to my cell burst inward and the "suits" flowed in. Poised to kill like a trapped wolverine, I gave the burly gang of thugs no other choice but to render me unconscious.

My senses reassembled inside a room that reminded me of a college dorm. The sterile confines contained two standard army-issue beds and a small, protruding closet in one corner that had obviously been included as an afterthought. To my relief, I turned and looked into the frightened eyes of a ghostly pale woman about my age: misery loves company!

As another woman walked past the window, a strong telepathic wave pressed into my mind: all three of us were captives, kidnapped as sacrificial lambs to be used for producing hybrids.

I was also told we were on Zeta Reticuli. I had no idea who or what was transmitting the thoughts, but I suspected they were lies. Nevertheless, I became so upset at that information I had a difficult time hearing the rest of the message.

I got the impression I would be punished by having an extended stay if I did not tell the complete truth about something they wanted to know. The voice scolded that not telling the entire truth was just as bad as lying. I didn't know what it was talking about, but I felt depressed and helpless, fearing my

invisible wardens were going to keep me indefinitely whether I cooperated or not.

Abruptly, reality rotated me onto a dark, surreal stage with only two high-backed chairs for props. A man with salt-and-pepper hair was engaged in conversation with a mutated hybrid being, who looked strangely like a foreign monarch seated in his plush, upholstered throne.

When the creature turned and looked in my direction, I became nauseous: one half of his face was terribly deformed. Even though I made sure not to reveal disgust on my face, the extraterrestrial's piercing insight immediately informed him how repulsive I found his appearance. His expression etched an archival imprint into the emulsion of my memory.

The alien responded telepathically that he knew a hybrid who was missing its entire upper lip, and that deformities of this nature were not uncommon in the crossbreeding of humans and Greys. ❤

It was apparent to me from this experience that the military and the aliens have an ongoing relationship. However, it soon became clear it might be one of mutual mistrust.

WARNING SIGNS
April 15, 1993

Dear Diary:

*I*t was one of those frustrating nights of tossing and
turning—something I've grown accustomed to. And
wouldn't you know it, someone decided I needed another
"acupuncture" adjustment. My body flinched. The prickling
sensation really annoyed me more than it hurt. I would have
fought to the death if only they had the guts to show their
cowardly, lifeless faces.

The paralysis came on stronger than ever before; it actually
made me sick to my stomach. This time it was accompanied by
a sensation of tremendous force that felt like it was going to
suck me through the bed and right through the floor. Once
again, I knew I was under someone else's control…I really
hate when that happens!

I resisted with everything I had, but I just wasn't strong
enough. I finally had to let go and fall into the vacuum.

Sometime later, I felt sensations returning here and there
throughout my body. I was conscious but totally paralyzed up
to my sealed eyelids. My back and legs were pressed against
what I assumed to be my bed.

My mind held a vision of people in a control booth. I could
see a window, a console, and the people behind it, but I had no

Warning Signs

sense of who they were or why they were interested in me. It was very creepy. The vision was interrupted when something grabbed my left hand. The fingers that clenched mine were strong, rough, and wrinkled.

As I lay traumatized, helpless, and blind, a tremendous weight crushed my torso, squeezing the breath right out of me. Whoever or whatever clutched my hand was now draped across my solar plexus.

Strong psychic messages burned into my mind. Suddenly, I knew my attacker was an older man, and the words "government agent" pulsed through my head. Finally, the lack of oxygen, or perhaps something else, knocked me out.

The foul odor of mildew and dust filled my nostrils. I was face down, my nose pressed into the seam of the back seat of an old sedan. The street lamps cast moving shadows into the windows as the car sped through a residential neighborhood. I lifted my drugged head up off the bench to take stock of the situation and realized I was the company of two plainclothes government men. The gorilla on the passenger side swung around and pushed my head back into the seat. "Stay down!" he growled. I took that as a hint he didn't want me looking around.

I desperately wanted to see out the window, so I kept bobbing

up and he kept pushing me back down. I rested a moment, pretending to be defeated, then sheepishly pulled my body into a sitting position, careful not to draw his attention.

What I saw was beyond belief. We were being chased by a disk! I immediately sensed the ship was trying to help me. A physical sign appeared beneath the craft which read, "Do Not Consume Food Or Alcohol Before Sleep." As if someone put a bag over my head, everything went black and that was the last thing I remember. ☻

I woke up in the morning feeling completely distraught. There was no clue as to what happened after I saw the sign, but I knew someone had really messed with my mind. I actually had suicidal thoughts all the next day, which is totally opposite my nature.

I called Darryl and told him I had to see him immediately. I didn't want to be alone because I was afraid I would do something stupid. He was at my doorstep in no time.

That afternoon we discussed the event and the meaning of the sign. Since I became aware of the fact I am being continually abducted, I have taken on a bad habit of eating food and drinking beer at night before I retire because it helps to sedate me. Knowing I'm being kidnapped from my bed makes it pretty hard to go to sleep at night. As a matter of fact, it's still the hardest thing I do every day of my life. We came to the conclusion the craft was trying to tell me I would have

more control over these devious situations if I didn't anesthetize myself first with food and alcohol.

The funny part is I usually overconsume to suppress my fear of being abducted by the *aliens*. This time, my abductors were human and aliens were my allies! Go figure.

This incident twisted the whole extraterrestrial enigma in another direction. I am certain our government is aware of the alien agenda and is withholding evidence, but the apparent extent of its involvement became extremely disturbing after the events which had occurred to me. I can understand the justification for hiding the truth from the masses—to prevent panic—but officials are obviously doing more than withholding information. They are participating, but it is difficult to determine whose side they are on.

There are a number of well-researched books that address the ongoing suspicions (which I believe to be based on fact) that the U.S. military retrieved a crashed UFO from the desert near Roswell, New Mexico, in 1947. Several of these works are listed in the appendix entitled "Suggested Reading," so I won't go into great detail here.

Suffice it to say that dozens of credible researchers, including scientists and retired Air Force personnel, have come forward and spoken publicly in recent years of their firsthand knowledge about this labyrinthine cover-up.

Most investigators give credence to the notion that members of the United States Government entered into an agreement

with the Greys sometime between 1947 and the end of the Eisenhower administration. The distilled and potent essence of this agreement was to allow the Greys to continue with their secret abductions so as to fulfill their own programs. In return for this "hands-off" policy, the government was to receive more alien technology, which would give it a great advantage toward insuring its own position of world supremacy.

I have seen humanoids working side by side with the aliens. Whether they were human beings or not, I am uncertain. The underground bases I've seen were, by all visible indications, of human construction. As a matter of fact, the buildings were all designed in the architectural style of the 1950s. I don't believe the aliens would take the trouble to fake such interiors.

The abduction by the government men was just as upsetting, if not more so, than any alien encounter. My emotional state the following day suggested I had been subjected to some kind of mental torment. Perhaps the government wanted to silence me. Convincing someone to commit suicide would be a clean way to do it.

Maybe the military suspects dishonesty in their alien associates, so they grab abductees and interrogate us to see if we know something they don't. I wish I knew the whole story; hopefully, time will tell all.

The central theme of the science-fiction film *They Live,* which came out several years ago, deals with aliens who come to Earth and covertly take over the planet with the help of

greedy humans. In return for their cooperation, the humans are rewarded handsomely. I'll bet viewers who saw it considered it to be on the furthest reaches of fantasy!

Technologies as profound as instantaneous space travel, manipulation of time, and total control over mind and matter are tempting toys for the power hungry.

But you would think that by being raised with "American morality" our government and military would not succumb to such underhanded dealings. How idealistic to think so.

However, we usually reap what we sow and, not surprisingly, there are indications that the government may have entered into a worthless contract on the basis of promised technologies which have been doled out in meager bits. Meanwhile, the Greys run rampant through our lives, most likely amused by our feeble, ineffective attempts to achieve a balance of power.

But this incident with the government threw in a whole new consideration. As much as I'd like to think so, I doubt that craft contained Greys. Who were the occupants that were trying to help me? Unfortunately, I may never know! ☻

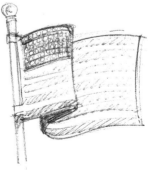

IN THE BLINK OF AN EYE
June, 1993

Dear Diary:

*y eyes followed the gentle curves of the tiny face
in hopes of capturing the time we'd lost.
Dim memories of stolen moments in this place,
wondering if she knew what her birth had cost.*

*My arms, a sanctuary for this perfect child of one.
Time's arrow flew swiftly toward a future scene.
My seed had blossomed like a flower in the sun.
In a single moment, she held the promise of thirteen.*

*Slender and delicate; a porcelain rose, glowing
with bright innocence, she watched with my own green eyes.
I desired to love her without showing
how much I missed having her in my life.*

*The fire of her intellect surpassed her emotional air,
which my maternal presence breathed into her spirit.
But she saw the heartbreak it causes to care,
imagined her own future child, and chose to fear it.*

*I gently reached out to soothe her fears
and reassured her from the depths of my soul
that even a moment with her was worth all the tears
and for her, like me, the love of a child would make her whole.*

Not that anything can justify how the aliens are intruding into our lives, but there's a saying, "Something good comes out of everything." This daughter, whom I named April, is the best thing to have come out of the alien design.

The extraterrestrial realm is not restricted to time as we know it. The night I spent with April defied that aspect of our reality entirely. One moment she was a tiny baby in my arms, the next moment she was standing before me as an adolescent with unmatchable intellect.

Though the memories are vacant, I realize I've had an ongoing relationship with this child. I was extremely bonded to her. I experienced the kind of love for her that my friends with children always talk about; that pure unconditional love you can only know as a parent.

She looked exactly like I did at that age and could have been a clone if it weren't for her frailer body and ivory skin. The strongest indication of her alien ancestry was her mental acuity. I could tell she knew many things I would never know, but there was no time to talk. In the brief moments we had together, all I wanted to do was love her and somehow compensate for all the time we had been deprived of. I fought back the tears, but I couldn't hide the pain of not being able to be there for her in those tender years. With her keen telepathy, she couldn't help but share my sorrow.

There are moments in just about every day when I see women with their children and I think about April. I know I am

Blink

missing out on the most wonderful thing in life, but the greatest pain is knowing how alone she must feel. In the short time we spent together, I recognized her emotions were as strong as any child's, but she is forced to live in a grey, emotionless desert with beings who don't understand the depth of a young girl's fears, hopes, and dreams. Every day I pray I am wrong. Perhaps the benefit of her advanced intelligence will counter-balance the absence of human interaction. I hope telepathy bypasses time and space so all the love I send her can, in part, make up for my not physically being there.

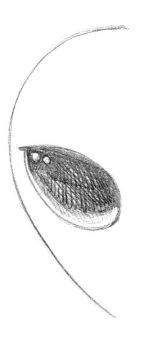

Beyond My Wildest Dreams

A MATTER OF PERSPECTIVE
Regression

Dear Diary:

I had a regression today. The clarity of the memory was astonishing. I could feel the temperature of the room, I could feel my physical surroundings, and I could feel my loathing for them as if I was really there.

When the memory began, I was sitting down, working at a computer. I had the unnerving feeling I was being watched. A voice inside my head said, "You're doing so well," and I turned around to discover one of those abominations staring over my shoulder like a diligent schoolmaster.

At his prodding, I halfheartedly operated a ball-like tracking device as a series of images flashed across the screen.

I didn't have a clue about the purpose of the exercise and I couldn't have cared less. I spun the ball aimlessly, reveling in my rebellion. Even so, the being was inanely patronizing, as though my actions were those of a genius.

The circular white room was sterile and barren, and I resented that the aliens had the power to rip me from my warm bed in the middle of the night to play this seemingly pointless game, and for whatever else they had in store for me.

I fumed with contempt and endured the procedure until the experience abruptly ended. 👽

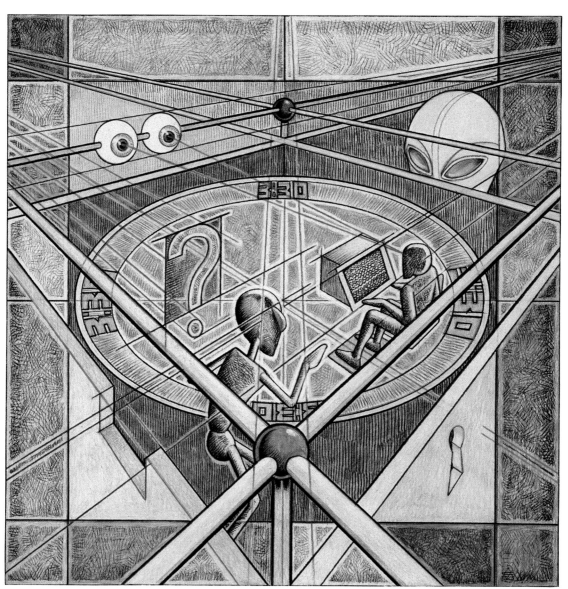

Perspective

THE ABYSS
July, 1993

Dear Diary:

I woke up to find myself floating along in a dark void next to a different kind of alien. He was between six and seven feet tall with dark, wrinkled skin. Although he was bald, his features were more human than the slick, uniform faces of the smaller Greys. His slanted, green cat eyes, big nose, and normal lips created a likable face.

I was so surprised by my lucidity, I asked the being if he was real. He replied "yes" and, as if to prove it, he applied a light kiss to my lips that carried a sweet compassion. I almost suspected that this being loved me, even though I had no idea who or what he was.

After drifting a while in ominous ether, we finally arrived at what felt like a dimensional barrier. The alien pushed me through the invisible membrane into a less-dense atmosphere, but he stayed behind. This new dimension had gravity, and I rapidly fell into the blackness of a bottomless pit. My mind was lost to the abyss.

When I came to, I was in a hospital ward so crowded with tables that the congestion reminded me of a M.A.S.H. unit. I could barely squeeze through the narrow aisles as I followed a "nurse" across the room. We passed a man strapped to a

The Abyss

table, who was awake and had been stripped down to only a T-shirt. Another "nurse" was doing something to his penis. I couldn't help but look at him and because I was so close, I brushed his body as I walked by. When he turned his head and looked away, I felt his humiliation. It made me heartsick to see him so helpless and embarrassed.

Then I realized my own plight and yelled at the nurse in front of me. "Don't you realize I'm totally conscious? Your mind tricks don't work on me anymore and I won't let you do this to me again! You've already ruined my body. I won't allow this to happen!"

The woman turned around and seemed to be sympathetic. She telepathically told me she was just a worker with no authority, so she couldn't just take me back home, but she could help me escape.

Talk about being lost! I had no idea even what planet I was on, or what dimension I was in. Finding my way home was really going to be a challenge, but nothing could be worse than being the focal point of their entertainment again. If there was a way out, I would gladly take it.

The nurse led me to a back door, opened it and, without saying a word, handed me a pair of shoes. I grabbed the shoes and ran through the cold, pitch-black night, turned a corner of the building, and felt my way along the back wall. A door swung open and an old hag nurse blocked my path. With her arms crossed arrogantly, "Nurse Ratchett" sarcastically

remarked, *"You thought you were going to get away, did you?"*

I couldn't believe a nurse could be so mean. I looked deep into her eyes searching for some kindness. I wanted her to understand I was truly a good person and she shouldn't be treating me this way. What a stupid move that was! Of course, connecting with her eyes gave her total power over me and I blacked out again. 👽

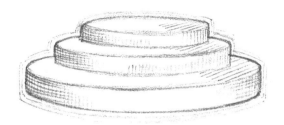

HERE'S MUD IN YOUR MOUTH
July, 1993

Dear Diary:

In total darkness I gagged on a mouthful of thick mud: its purpose, to steady the hose that crawled down my throat like a rubber centipede. My muscles tightened to grip the penetrating probe, but to no avail.

As the tube wormed its way deeper and deeper into my gut, my unexpressed question, "How could this be happening?" was taken literally by my hidden tormentors as a technological query, and an illustration of the mechanics of the hose was diagrammed into my psyche in vivid detail.

The tube had smaller shafts inside, so when the first section got to a part of my throat that was too narrow for it to pass, a smaller cylinder would telescope out and go down even further.

I've had this same "dream" more times than I care to remember. ☻

BIOLOGICAL IDENTITY

PROJECT BLUE BOOK

theories and phenomena

Mud

TWO SIDES OF THE SAME STORY
November 3, 1993

Dear Diary:

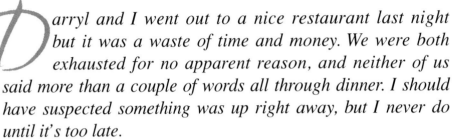

arryl and I went out to a nice restaurant last night but it was a waste of time and money. We were both exhausted for no apparent reason, and neither of us said more than a couple of words all through dinner. I should have suspected something was up right away, but I never do until it's too late.

I made it home as quickly as possible, obsessed with the idea of sleep. On my way to bed, I passed the UFO sketches on the dining table which Darryl had been working on all day for the book. As I did, I started humming along with a mysterious sound that was playing inside my mind. I thought I recognized it as a noise I had heard coming from a craft, and wondered if the sketches might have triggered an unconscious memory.

When I lay down, I realized the whirring sound I had been imitating was still running through my head, and it would not go away. I sat back up and covered my ears to see if it was coming from the inside or the outside of my head, but I couldn't decide; the sound seemed to be everywhere.

Then I realized: of course! It always happens the same way but I never recognize the symptoms until after the fact. I usually become inordinately exhausted hours before an abduction. It is

one of the little tricks they use to get me into bed to relax or sleep so they can do their dirty deeds.

I still wanted to believe the noise was just a figment of my imagination, so I convinced myself it couldn't be them because it was only 10:00 P.M. They are night stalkers and never strike until the early morning hours when the world is asleep and unguarded. I muffled the sound with some mental affirmations and went into a light slumber.

I slept for a short while but woke to the whirring sound, which had increased in volume. My mouth was parched and in my mind was a three-dimensional picture of the water bottle in the kitchen refrigerator. I was confused because there was a water bottle less than two feet from my head on the floor near the bed; but, by the time I put two and two together, my hand was already on the refrigerator door. Suddenly it felt like the ice water I was reaching for was already running through my veins; the aliens were in the dark only a few feet away! I couldn't believe I fell for the aliens' trick so quickly. The picture of the water bottle in my head, along with the thirst, had been psychic projections.

I swung around to run for my life, but my body froze in mid-air like a frame from a cartoon strip. One foot was completely off the ground, and both arms were hurled in opposite directions. I was suspended, completely immobilized, but my thinking was clear. There was only one thing I could do. I focused all of my concentration and screamed "No!" at the top of my lungs. I broke

free and the presence left. I was amazed the neighbors didn't call the cops.

It felt great to win a small battle, but I knew it wasn't over. It seems the aliens have a schedule to keep and if it's your night, they persist until sunrise. The tenacious predators would wait until I fell back asleep and try another approach.

I'm not sure why they endeavored to capture me from the kitchen instead of my bed this time, but I suspect they know my subconscious is becoming wise to them since I have been able to wake up and resist recent abduction attempts. I guess they thought this new approach would catch me off guard and be more effective. Sorry fellows!

I tried to stay awake the rest of the night, since that's the only thing that ever works against them. I ate candy, hoping a sugar buzz would keep me alert.

At 11:00 P.M., my friend Cheri called. A few weeks ago, she finally figured out that several of the bizarre and unexplainable occurrences throughout her life had actually been abductions. She lives only a few blocks away and wanted to know if I "felt" anything because she sensed the aliens "lurking." She was pretty upset. It was interesting to finally see my shoes on someone else's feet. I tried to comfort her even though I was panicked myself. I assured her with simple logic that she would be all right. "We've been through this before and we're still here, aren't we?" When she was mollified, I called Darryl; I needed calming myself. He was as sweet as always, and he kept talking to keep

me awake until he could think of nothing else to say.

When we hung up, I left all the lights on, propped my body up with pillows, and conjured up images of gnarly wolves perched around me on the bed. I was hoping if I endowed my thought projections with enough energy, it would bring the wolves to life and they would eat any intruding Zetas. When you're desperate you'll try anything. Unfortunately it didn't work.

The prickling started at my feet and moved up my body, like a thousand needles being applied over and over again. I hated the sensation, not so much for how it felt, but for what it meant: they *were back. My head started swirling and I quickly lost consciousness.*

When I woke up, I was alone in the living room of a small house and could see through the open front door that it was as dark outside as it was inside. Gravitating to the door, I observed a group of people standing in the yard, spellbound by something in the sky. I exited the house to see what all the excitement was about and recognized a rectangular craft with running lights on two sides, zigzagging across the sky.

The group was oblivious to the danger they were in, so I informed them. "Run for your lives! They are not friendly. They will capture you!" We all took off together down the street, turned the first corner, and came to a dead standstill in front of a fantastic vision. We were face to face with a glamorous fleet of shimmering spacecraft. Two different groups, side by side, emanated from the horizon, separated by an enormous cloud

formation that seemed to be cloaking something within it. There were literally hundreds of ships.

A distinctly different psychic mood radiated from each of the two groups of craft. The bell-like craft seemed uninterested, apathetic, along for the ride, while the football-shaped ships projected authority and concern. Our group stood totally speechless, in absolute awe.

I slowly emerged from my "dream" still very much in awe. It was 3:30 A.M. What I witnessed had been a humbling experience, to say the least. I don't know if it was a real experience, a holographic projection, or another one of their psychic manipulations. Then again, it may have been a simple aberration of my own mind. I have given up trying to tell the difference, but I think I'm beginning to understand what the yogis have always known: life is really a dream and dreams are real. An enlightened soul realizes there is no difference.

I do not know the purpose of this event. It seems to me, after all these years of cat and mouse and meaningless riddles, they would tire of the game and leave or come closer, but the game remains the same: a mystery. 👽

Researchers suspect abduction is generational, passing from parents to children. The aliens apparently prefer to follow familiar bloodlines and start gathering the genetic information beginning at birth. Sometimes they even begin before birth.

Two Sides

Another female abductee I know told me about abductions she had during her pregnancy when the aliens showed her the developing baby on a screen, revealing its gender.

My friend Cheri was sure her son and granddaughter were involved, and she wanted me to meet her two-year-old granddaughter, Opal. There is nothing more heart-wrenching than hearing a two year old talk about the "bad doctors" who come in the night.

I was shooting some copy work in my home when Opal came to meet me. I use strobes for lighting and when I released the shutter, discharging the strobes, Opal ran to her grandmother and hid her little face in Cheri's lap for ten minutes. The flashing light had scared her to death, far beyond any normal reaction. I have photographed children with strobes for years, and I had never seen a response like this. Flashing lights are common in abduction, from the craft and in the examination chambers.

Meeting Opal convinced me that writing a book was necessary. Though I am no scholar and have no credentials, every contribution adds to the validity of the subject. Perhaps Opal will grow up in a world more informed and less rejecting, when her generation speaks about the alien "harvesters."

UNDER CONSTRUCTION
Conscious Abduction
November 8, 1993

Dear Diary:

I went to bed and fell asleep like any ordinary night (as if there was such a thing) but later woke up to someone or something putting me back into my bed. A being held me like a baby in its skinny arms, then gently rolled me onto my side.

I lay there trying to move anything, but my efforts to even wiggle a toe were fruitless. My body felt like a ton of steel. I attempted the technique that had worked in the past, moving my head from side to side until the paralysis ceased, but even that was too much effort. Opening my eyes was the best I could do. The room was empty; it was 3:10 A.M. I gave up trying to stimulate my muscles and decided to just sleep it off.

A moment later my eyes popped open to see a figure with a black hood standing at the foot of my bed. I almost laughed. It was such a cliché: the famous hooded figure. But my name wasn't Scrooge, and it definitely wasn't Christmas.

I stared into the shroud trying to find a face inside the darkness, but to no avail. As if it sensed my disappointment, the "grim reaper" transformed before my very eyes. It became something with which it thought I could easily identify: of all things, a construction worker, perfect in every detail with a

flannel shirt, jeans, tan leather boots, and matching tool belt. The chiseled face was that of a man in his thirties with a short beard and moustache. The next instant I was floating weightlessly beside him. He had come for me, and for some reason I had no thoughts of resisting. I followed like an eager puppy. As we passed through the closet doors, I was embarrassed by the ridiculous questions that escaped my mouth.

"Are you human?"

"Of course," he responded.

"So how did you move through those solid doors?"

He chuckled as we both realized the absurdity of my question. I barely noticed that I, myself, had just accomplished the same feat, exactly the way the Greys had entered my room almost one year before.

From the closet, we passed into solid blackness. I was only aware of movement, until some dim source provided me with enough light to see we were gliding down a cement ramp into a basement or underground level of a building.

At the end of the ramp was a group of more "construction workers." I turned around, looked over their heads to ground level and saw a towering, pyramidal structure. My mind was trying to say "Luxor Hotel" but instead, my lips uttered, "Oh, this must be Caesar's Palace." They were all amused. The tallest one put his hand on my face, and all my curiosity subsided.

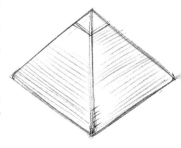

I felt warm and relaxed, as if I had taken a Valium. With glazed eyes, I looked at him and said, "Gee, I can't wait until I

have the power to do that." Contented, I turned and continued to follow my original guide and, as soon as we passed through a set of glass doors, I saw my former boyfriend, David. He looked miserable and his movements and speech were lethargic. "They slowed my motor cortex," he explained. Poor David was having so much difficulty walking and was in so much pain, it made me cry. I put my arms around his neck and hugged him.

As if I was connected by a psychic leash, the construction worker tugged at me and I obediently followed him up a small flight of stairs. We passed a large, cylindrical tank containing two babies floating upside down in a watery liquid. I was astonished they were so perfectly formed and healthy looking. Each had Caucasian skin, but one had black, curly hair while the other had soft, red hair. I ran past them as quickly as possible. I couldn't stand any more baby stuff.

Then, to my surprise, I started recognizing the place as if I'd been there many times before, but the specific memories were missing. I was so excited I was totally conscious and everything was so clear. My chaperone released me and I ran wildly through the complex, remembering everything: rest rooms, classrooms, the cafeteria, etc. I was overjoyed I was awake, aware, and free to roam this place that was as familiar as a second home.

Just when I thought maybe the visit wasn't going to be as awful as most, someone came and took me to the place I recognized as the "bad" room! I immediately felt ill as I was

forced through the door, because I knew that the most horrible things occurred in there. Then I blacked out.

I reawakened mid-stride, walking out of the "bad" room. I was immediately suspicious because I was fully dressed in street clothes and carrying a handbag.

A moment later, my friend Michael walked by. I could tell he had been drugged and he looked awful. He stopped and said, "They keep bringing me back to drain this," as he pointed to his face. I looked closely. I wasn't sure what he had pointed to, but the smell of clinical alcohol coming from his skin made me queasy.

Simultaneously, we looked at an unguarded door and I knew we were both thinking the same thing: escape! As we approached the door, we were casually joined by two other humans, and I knew we all had the same objective: to get the hell out of there. It was very dark outside, but I felt something guiding me, which should have been a red alert.

We walked around to the side of the building where there was a large parking lot with one car and one "parking lot attendant" who was leaning on the automobile. When I looked into the face of the attendant, I knew something peculiar was going on. He was intensely focused on me alone.

A telepathic voice told me the keys to the car were inside the purse and if I wanted to escape, I had to hurry. But more than hearing words, I felt an energy with them that was overwhelmingly convincing. My adrenaline pumped!

Under Construction

I pulled the keys from the purse and nonchalantly went for the handle of the car, as if the vehicle belonged to me. The attendant intentionally blocked my path, demanding my name.

The voice in my mind continued. "You can't tell him your name; he can look it up on the computer inside and he'll know you're an abductee trying to escape. You will have to try another approach."

I followed the instructions and, looking into his eyes with the sweetest sincerity I could evoke, I tried flattery, "You know, you look just like John Lennon!" He chuckled and sent me a thought. "You're trying to butter me up." Instantly, I started getting groggy as someone grabbed me by the arm and led me back into the building. As my head cleared, I realized I was on my way to another "bad" room.

I emerged from the second room, sluggish from whatever method of mistreatment had been swept from my memory. Clarity was instantly thrust upon me like a razor-cut. Rivers of fire flowed up my arms and legs, drowning my senses in excruciating pain. The palms of my hands were raw with open wounds, and the skin on my legs was red where the top layers had been stripped off.

A heavy, black woman stood by the door as if she worked there. I pleaded with her for some understanding. "What sort of people could allow these kinds of things to go on?"

"I don't know" was her only response.

I was suddenly back in my bed. My body buzzed. I flipped

the light on and yanked my gown up to examine the tops of my legs. The wounds were still there! I sat staring at the holes in my hands in agony and disbelief, but before my very eyes, the wounds started healing. It was like watching a high speed film of clouds moving, or like a segment of a nature film that shows the gestation or lifetime of a plant or animal in a matter of seconds. The whole process lasted no more than two minutes. The clock read 5:14 A.M. 👽

These are two mild examples of the types of "studies" the aliens carry out. Escape and rescue are their favorite themes. This simple escape scenario, with the "parking lot attendant," tested my ability to think my way out of a situation. Most others have involved more physical pursuit, like being chased by people wielding weapons.

I suspect the two other humans who followed us out the door weren't human at all. They were probably aliens in disguise. That would explain the guiding voice and arm that grabbed me and took me back inside.

I do not fully comprehend the symbology of the black robed figure, although it rouses many intriguing ideas. Nevertheless, there was a lot of obvious meaning behind the way they chose to present themselves as construction workers. I wonder if they were telling me that is how they see themselves—as the "labor force" behind human evolution.

Pain threshold is another one of their special interests. On other occasions, I have been purposely subjected to intense physical pain, to the point of passing out as the aliens observed with detachment. At least this time I healed quickly.

I've wondered if the torture is intentional. Our intellect may be so dense that the only way to break through to us is to break us down, and what more effective way to do that than to get us where we live; in our bodies. Nothing is as inescapable in my life as physical pain. Psychological pain is more transmutable. A smart mind can talk its way out of an uncomfortable mind-set.

Nothing is as humbling as being constantly rendered helpless by a species of much greater intelligence and technology. To be treated again and again like a frog in a science class, and then completely ignored while crying out in agony, allows abductees to see themselves and humanity in a completely different light. Our arrogance about ourselves becomes laughable, and one is forced to reevaluate where we fit in the hierarchy of life.

Perhaps the aliens are a portion of our own consciousness from the future that has come back, not to "housebreak" but more appropriately to "Earthbreak" us bad humans.

I have been drugged, strapped to a table, and used for my capacity to reproduce; treated with no more respect than a

machine; and looked upon like I existed for nothing more than their consumption. Sound familiar? Sometimes I could almost hear the Greys say, "What's the matter? You do the same thing to the animals on your Earth. You don't like it, do you?" What better way to stop an ego-bound species from unconsciousness and inhumanity than by reversing the roles.

Maybe they are some kind of alter ego, physically mirroring a statement that cannot be delivered any other way. They definitely reflected a portion of myself I did not want to see: such as how unemotional and disconnected I had become from my own world, particularly from such species as plants and insects that I considered to be less than myself.

The extraterrestrials say, "You are us," but what does this mean? Surely, if they were me, they would feel the horror I experience during an abduction and change their tactics or leave me alone altogether, unless their purpose is so great they cannot take the time to consider the effects they are having on their victims. I have watched them work in fury, racing against time—not their time, but our time. Collecting what they can of human DNA before we suffer from complete ecological collapse might be a big enough goal.

Whether it was the Greys' intention to tame me or not, they did. My values have changed dramatically over the course of my involvement with them. Material gain has lost its meaning. My relationships are now my highest priority, whether it be with people, the planet, or that which I term "All That Is." I am

a much kinder person today and I hate to admit it, but I owe a lot of my new attitude to the aliens.

I have had the opportunity to view human nature through their eyes, and it has been an enlightening journey. I look at the violence in which modern man is constantly engaged and question what the aliens must think. No wonder they treat us the way they do. How could we possibly have the respect of an alien race when we don't have respect for our own, or, for that matter, for the very Earth on which our lives depend.

As much as I hate the extraterrestrials, I can no longer say they are evil. I realize "hate" is a strong word and I am not a hateful person. I do not truly hate anyone or anything, but vocabulary is limiting.

If I do have an emotion close to "hate," it is for circumstances that are beyond my control, such as the aliens choosing me. I resent that they are constantly inflicting physical and psychological pain with no regard for my well-being.

But love and hate are two sides of the same coin, and my link with the aliens is the epitome of a love/hate relationship.

Setting aside their monstrous methodologies, the aliens have taught me invaluable lessons. They have shown me that not only does everything have consciousness, everything *is* consciousness. We are more than the material forms we embody, yet our encasements are also born from spirit. The animals, plants, insects, and Earth itself are conscious, living beings, and we are all connected very literally by the same energy.

The words vex my mind like a festering splinter I cannot dig out: "You are us." Although I would rather deny it, I know it is the ultimate truth.

It seems this self of which we are all a part—God if you will—is trying to reconnect on a biological, as well as spiritual, level. I fantasize that God, like God's creations, may also dream and may be attempting to achieve a state of lucid dreaming or heightened consciousness, just as we strive to become more aware of our own total selves. Perhaps the moments in which this Creator reaches new levels of awareness give rise to our human religious experiences and flashes of revelations.

Attempting to obtain a state of total consciousness is a difficult undertaking for any being, whether it be the Creator or the created, because the fragments of the self fear each other. They suspect they may face a part of themselves they would rather reject, the same way I would rather reject the Greys. The separate aspects feel that acknowledging each other will bring about the loss of individuality, the loss of self. Dark secrets would be exposed. The irony is that, as much as we try to hide from one another, it is futile. On deeper levels, we always know the truth.

I believe telepathy is the most natural form of communication, but is rare in our civilization because we are so afraid to be who we are; we're afraid to be honest. In my experience, telepathy is easiest with people who have no lies to conceal. Therefore, if a society is to become joined telepathically, it must be of the highest integrity.

It's a shame to allow fear to stand in the way of the joy and wholeness that is available when we allow ourselves to connect, whether it be with other people, mother nature, aliens, or God. That moment I was shown "You Are Us" was the most profound event in my life, but I don't believe it has to be limited to a single moment.

Consciousness is seeking to know itself. The time has come for us to open our eyes to that "One" energy, to evolve our thinking about who *we* are to include all things, from the smallest atom to a fleet of motherships, from the hardest stone to the finest vibrations of nonphysical realities. When our thinking expands about who and what we are as a consciousness, all other parts of the whole will reflect that knowing.

The things we consider "outside" of ourselves are always speaking to us, but their voices can only be heard with the heart. If you say "hello" to a tree, you may not hear a "hello," but you may be surprised. You may just hear the echo of a raindrop, or a snowflake landing on a leaf, and find yourself observing the precious give-and-take between them that allows life to continue. Perhaps you would sense the safety felt by all the little creatures who find solace in the arms of the tree. Then you might reconsider before you axe down its sister for a Christmas ornament!

We are young as species go. We still have a lot of evolving to do and can start by chopping away at our own self-centeredness and limited, outdated worldview.

When humanity surrenders to the knowledge that we are not alone in the universe, and ceases to deny the existence of other forces, we can allow those forces to surface. Until then, the aliens are doing what our fear demands they do: remain in hiding.

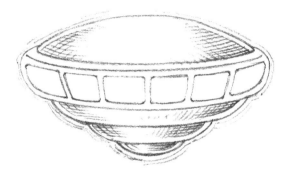

I am now usually aware when an abduction is about to take place. I fight every time it begins, and I am able to stop it more and more as time goes on, but I am not always successful. Maybe someday I will learn how to fend off the Greys for good, but, for now, not only are the abductions continuing, they seem to be contagious.

I recently spent the night in the guest room at Darryl's house near Los Angeles. It was a couple of weeks after the 6.8 quake of January 1994. Darryl and his wife, Erica, were in their room, right down the hall.

I dozed off, but awoke to a whirring sound. I got out of bed and peeked through Darryl and Erica's door to see if they heard it too, but found them sleeping peacefully. I didn't have the heart to wake them. With all the shaking from the constant aftershocks, we were all exhausted. I tiptoed around the house looking out every window to see where the noise was coming from, but found nothing. Of course, I couldn't see directly above the house, but I was too afraid to go outside and look up. I went back to bed and lay there in dread. Just as I suspected, a few moments later the paralysis struck. I battled to maintain consciousness, and in my mind I screamed for Darryl to save me.

Seconds later, the bedroom door swung open. "Kim, are you all right?" *They* released their grip; I could move. "Darryl, I was

calling out to you telepathically and you heard me!"

Darryl interrupted, "I felt it, I felt the paralysis! Now I know what you've been talking about all this time! I knew you were in trouble, and I broke free of it!"

We stayed up talking about the incident for another hour but we were both so tired we had to try and get some sleep. Later that night, an abduction did occur. I was put through one of the typical pursuits that tested my problem-solving abilities. I did not see anyone else during that experience, and the next morning Darryl could not recall anything unusual about the rest of the night.

Two weeks later, Darryl came over to tell me about a "dream" he had. "I was in a dim place," he explained. "A beautiful little blond girl with big blue eyes, who I estimated to be about seven years old, stood in front of me with a blue thermometer in her mouth. I saw a hand on her shoulder and I knew it was a nurse. I took the child into my arms to comfort her because she was sick, and I 'felt' a thought or an energy come from the nurse that said, 'That's right, that's what she needs.' I continued to comfort the child I knew was your daughter, then out of the darkness you came up from behind and put your arms around us both."

Maybe it was just a dream, or maybe the abduction phenomenon spreads to those you love and who love you. If this is

true, the hybrid children have a good chance of fully realizing the most significant attribute of their human lineage, love, and taking it with them wherever their destinies lead.

Just in case it's not obvious by now, I want to make it perfectly clear that I truly despise the aliens for abducting me. But, as I have said throughout this work, I do appreciate the way my consciousness has been stretched through the process of my encounters with them. When one knows beyond a shadow of a doubt other realms exist, it changes a person's beliefs about what is possible.

One of the first telling signs an abduction is about to occur is a telepathic linkup. Unfortunately for the ETs, and also thanks to them, my ESP has expanded to the point that, when they think about me, I know it. This supports the idea that thoughts travel long distances instantly. Telepathy seems to be the universal language, and because it is not limited to space/time, it also opens up a plethora of opportunities for communication with many types of beings other than Grey aliens. Intrigued by the possibilities, I have been doing some experimenting and have had some pretty incredible experiences.

SHAPESHIFTER
January 4, 1994

Dear Diary:

or some reason I woke up at 4:30 A.M. without the usual sense of dread that accompanies most early awakenings. Nevertheless, I surveyed my home for anything suspicious. The house was uncommonly peaceful. I checked myself: no physical pain, none of the typical tingling sensations, no residual nightmare imagery of operating tables. Everything seemed undisturbed...that in itself was unusual.

Since I had retired at a relatively decent hour, I knew I wouldn't be able to get back to sleep. It was too early to start my day, and as I walked around the house looking for something to do, I had a sudden desire to meditate. The urge to quiet my mind was so strong I wondered if it wasn't originating from someone or something else. What better thing to do at 4:30 A.M. than to take a journey into consciousness.

I sat down on my bed, closed my eyes, and within a few seconds a subtle vibration moved upward through my body. Surprisingly, it didn't frighten me. It wasn't the same "abduction vibration" I know so well, therefore I chose not to fight it; my curiosity had the best of me. Time held its breath and, the next instant, I was standing in the entry hall of an empty house. The walls were unpainted and the place was dimly lit. It had the

feeling of a movie set; artificial and temporary, but it was a very real physical place. The front door blew open to reveal an ordinary suburban environment. A nicely manicured lawn and paved road were suddenly obscured by a dark, ominous form that resembled a spacecraft.

Panic set in and I instantly felt like a fool for not initially fighting the vibration. I guess they *fooled me again! At that moment, an open coat closet in the hall looked very inviting. I ran in, slammed the door behind me, curled up in the corner, and felt around for a mouse hole to crawl into. I was so scared I took the only thing in the closet, a six-inch square scarf, and covered my head, hoping that it would conceal me.*

A moment later, I was standing back in front of the door as if I experienced a glitch in time and had gone backward five minutes. The ship was still there, but its behavior was so mesmerizing I forgot my fear. I stood and stared as the craft started changing its shape. It remained black and foreboding, as if it belonged in the movie Star Wars *as a vehicle of the "Dark Side," but its outline would shift from square to oblong to oval in constant motion like an organic, breathing life-form.*

What happened next was far more spectacular than any production a Grey could muster, and I realized the extravaganza I was witnessing wasn't anything I had ever encountered before!

The undulating, animate thing relaxed its structure, stretched out its wings, and took flight. It moved through the air, further transforming into a tide of pure energy, and rushed

toward me. I fell back to witness the most miraculous sight! The astounding, formless entity blossomed into a dozen perfect bodies. Each face was a flawless sculpture of curiosity, and I knew the being chose the human images to facilitate communication. The young adults appeared to be in their mid-twenties and looked like characters you would see on Los Angeles' trendy Melrose Avenue. All were artistic types with unconventional hair styles and hip clothes. I think the entity was picking up on my identity as an artist and projecting it back to me physically. They were definitely kids I could relate to.

Patterns of nonverbal communication danced between us. My questions were answered before I could finish the thoughts, but I needed to hear my own voice to verify my experience. "I know what you are, you're a shapeshifter," I announced, directing my words to the young man on the end.

"That's correct," he said sweetly.

I was so excited I couldn't contain myself. "So will I ever evolve to be like you?" I directed my question to one of the females and realized, no matter which face I spoke to, I was addressing one being, one consciousness.

"You will never be like me, we are not the same."

Of course, I was disappointed by the answer but another question immediately jumped from my lips. "What is your natural form?"

The same male responded, "You would recognize it as something similar to your liquids."

Then it was my turn to answer the questions. A female, with her head tilted to one side and looking very confused, asked, "Why do the females of your species love more?" Every word and expression was infused with total, unconditional love. The innocence and sincere interest in her query brought me to tears.

My voice quivered as I explained, "It's not that we love more, it is simply a condition in our society that men do not express affection as easily as women."

Her eyes lit up and twinkled. "I see," she responded joyfully, and I knew she fully comprehended.

We stood in silence briefly, then I received an idea that there weren't very many of its kind in the universe. Another thought caressed my mind, and I realized it was time for the being to go. The communications were not verbal; they weren't even words inside my mind, which is the way telepathy occurs when I'm with the Greys. They were instant "knowings." It was the most efficient mode of exchanging information I've experienced thus far.

We shared mutual admiration and appreciation for the interaction, and I felt the most tender, pure love I think I have ever known. I walked up to each one of the physical representations and hugged them goodbye. Tears flowed down all of our faces and, as I held the last girl in my arms, she said, "If this is what it feels like to be human, I don't know if I want to do this again." I knew she was referring to the pain of separation, and I explained that it wasn't a negative thing to feel bad when

Shape Shifter

saying goodbye, that it only meant you loved that person all the more.

They formed a straight line at the door and, as the first male stepped over the threshold, his physical body became fluid. He then pulled the other bodies into the river of light he had just become. Once again in the form of pure energy, the being flowed to the street, regained the shape of a craft, and zipped away.

I was suddenly aware of my body sitting on my bed vibrating like a guitar string that had just been plucked. I jumped off the bed bubbling with energy and excitement, and ran around the house like I had just won the million-dollar lottery. The clock read 5:30 A.M. 👽

I grabbed the phone and called Darryl. I normally would not bother him at such an inappropriate hour, not even after an abduction. It's not that he would have minded, but his wife worked and I was always respectful not to disturb her sleep. However, this was more amazing than anything I'd experienced in all my years of extraordinary encounters and it begged to be shared.

Darryl woke from a deep sleep and I unloaded the whole story without taking a breath. When I finished he said, "I know you don't watch much television, Kim, but have you ever seen

Deep Space Nine?

"You know I've never seen it, Darryl."

"That's what I thought. This is very strange," he replied.

"What's strange?"

"Well...there is a reoccurring character on the show that is a shapeshifter."

"Really," I responded, a little disappointed. (I thought I had just discovered something totally new in the universe.) "What is it like?"

"This is really weird," Darryl kept insisting. "In the show, its natural state is liquid."

I was beginning to get goose bumps. "Yeah, what else?"

"You're not going to believe this...but on *Deep Space,* the being, named 'Odo,' claims there aren't many of his kind in the universe."

We hung up, and I wondered about the meaning of it all. Could I have possibly seen this program and not remembered? I played with the idea I might have had some sort of multiple personality disorder which allowed one "Kim" a sedate life of simple pleasures, like watching television, that the other, strict, success-oriented personality could never consider as a viable pastime. This thought churned up a lot of concern. I became frantic. I scrutinized my memory...there were obviously other events that had gone "unknown" in my life, like many of my abductions. Perhaps my mind had been told to forget so many times by the aliens that it had become overly efficient, creating

and applying its own computer programming. If so, maybe some secret longing deep within me, which desperately wanted to believe other, kinder beings than the Greys existed, had fabricated a dazzling delusion.

I paced. *Deep Space Nine*...I knew about the series, I'd heard the name several times, but I had no memory of ever seeing it. I replayed the elegant encounter in my mind again. I was sure it had been real! The emotion of it was rich beyond compare. Even if I had seen this character "Odo" on a TV show, which I was sure I hadn't, I doubted my mundane imagination could have conjured such a convincing performance as the shapeshifter displayed.

I pressed my memory further, but all that surfaced were images from the original *Star Trek* of my childhood. I have considered many times how similar some of the details of my abductions were to things I had seen during my youthful years of admiring Spock. Why had I found him so fascinating? Possibly, even as a child, a part of me understood the hidden significance of a make-believe character half human and half from another race, a creature void of emotion. I vaguely remember Spock bringing someone down with the "Vulcan nerve pinch," suspiciously similar to the slap on the neck I received from the tall Grey in my first conscious abduction. "Mind meld" and "transportation beam" were terms uncomfortably familiar to me, even when I heard them the first time.

Where do these ideas come from? Working in the movie

business myself, I know much, if not most, of the material in movies and television is based in reality. *BayWatch,* for example, came from Greg's own life experience. Why should science fiction be different? Several of my personal friends are writers. Rarely when discussing my abductions do I walk away without hearing, "That would make a great screenplay!"

Star Trek and *Deep Space Nine* accept outside scripts. That means anyone with an idea and the patience to put it to paper can submit a story for consideration. I know a number of people who have done so. I now believe the creator of "Spock" and the creator of "Odo" were drawing from personal insight or experience, conscious or unconscious, of very real beings. One could quite possibly have been the same entity I encountered at 4:30 A.M. on January 4, 1994.

Although I have seen beings change form in my presence before, such as the hooded figure changing into a construction worker, the shapeshifter was very different. I believe the hooded figure was an alien performing some sort of perceptual illusion. I'm sure "shapeshifting" is this new entity's true nature, rather than a trick it can do.

In the latter part of 1993, my friend Cheri, who is also a contactee, decided to change her vocation from that of a gourmet vegetarian chef to a hypnotherapist. Her initial interests had been typical: weight loss, stress reduction, and behavioral modification. She had already taken the appropriate schooling to become a hypnotherapist before realizing her own involvement with the aliens, and ended up on my hypnotherapist's couch just weeks after becoming one herself. Making appointments with Yvonne was difficult since she was highly sought after, and Cheri immediately realized the need for more qualified persons to assist abductees.

Cheri urged me to become certified myself because of all my personal knowledge on the subject. I considered it for a couple of days but decided it definitely wasn't my cup of tea. My life was totally absorbed with abduction. I was already spending most of my spare time helping "newly aware" abductees adjust. I definitely didn't want to do it full time. Besides, I loved my commercial photography career. It was exciting, creative, and paid well, so I wasn't interested in pursuing another career—at least not then.

THE PERSUADER
January, 1994

Dear Diary:

The universe is a very complex and crowded place, and becoming more so all the time. I woke up into an experience that had all the qualities of an abduction, but who orchestrated it is beyond my guess. I don't believe it was my old "traveling companions."

I gained consciousness in the middle of fighting to free my body from the invisible glue which stuck me to a wooden chair. My arms and legs were uncrossed, and my head was frozen in a forward position. I couldn't turn around to see, but something was definitely behind me.

An authoritative boom rang out, "How long would it take you to be certified as a hypnotherapist?"

I couldn't believe my ears! What kind of question was that? There I sat, whisked away in the middle of the night, paralyzed and bound to a chair, locked away in a dark cavity and someone was asking me about a certificate? I so much wanted to be able to move my fingers so I could pinch myself.

"Not long," I replied, not believing I was actually engaging in the absurd conversation. I felt something move up closer to my left, but it remained out of sight. A series of psychic brush strokes painted an impression on my imagination. It was the

image of a tall, lanky creature, somewhere between seven and nine feet and composed of light within an indistinct humanoid contour. The entity approached unencumbered by gravity, and a soft but stern resonance penetrated my ear, emphasizing every word independently. "Do…you…know…how…many…people …you…could…help?"

I knew it was a rhetorical question and contemplated it seriously before a surge of energy burst through my cells and I recognized the "ride" home—an eternal moment of knowing myself to be everything and nothing. My persona returned. I was sprawled on my bed, waiting for the molecules of my body to reorganize, when I decided it was probably in my best interest to heed the prospect put to me, instead of being my naturally stubborn self. The intensity in each word spoken by the entity was born from a source of great concern, and I couldn't help but take it to heart. 👽

Just who or what this being was has remained forever in the now-overflowing "Unsolved" file. I had not seen it with my physical eyes, but only with my mind's eye. Could it have been a sympathetic renegade Grey? Not likely…sympathetic and Grey are contradictions in terms.

The label "spirit guide" is cliché, but most likely an appropriate one in this case. But *spirit influence* is usually dispensed as *inspiration*; feelings or ideas that drop in with supernatural

Persuader

potency. I've yet to hear described an unilluminated pit with a wooden chair as the seat of divine counsel. Or physical paralysis by etheric beings with symphonic voices as necessary components for holy advice. As I returned to questioning the being's intentions, a voice from a childhood story echoed within me, "Are you a good witch or a bad witch?"

My life is now constantly barraged by omnipotent beings, and I gave up the quest to decipher good from evil long ago. I am becoming too small, too ignorant, in the face of such a vast universe to make such judgments. The more information and experiences I accumulate, the less I know. I gave up on logic: it became outdated hardware. I now resort to the only thing that continually pulls me through: instinct. I've discovered intellect and intelligence are light years from one another. Intelligence is present in all things, accessible from anywhere through one door: belief, faith, instinct, whatever name you choose. I double-checked my intuition and concluded the advice to get certified was coming from a high source—but something was missing.

I asked for guidance a thousand times and when I finally received it, I was a little disappointed. It certainly wasn't what I expected; it absolutely lacked the mystical wrapping I had envisioned. The instructions were anything but grandiose. Is this all the heavens expect of me? The One Above has always known I have much loftier ambitions, such as changing the world! That's the goal that motivates me. I must admit I feel

profoundly inadequate to the task, but still I find myself seeking an Earth I've seen in a vision.

I've walked this Earth in a "dream," where humankind has relinquished fear-induced addiction to control the very elements that created it. I came to a valley, where the only signs of fading domination are small gardens where vegetables are grown without poisons. There, people trust that the herbs Mother Earth sows are adequate measures for healing the few diseases which remained once they went back to living harmoniously with nature.

I breathed deeply into my lungs the sweet air of a pristine forest where the lives of trees are not cut short by greedy industry. I've dipped my toes into rivers that have been freed from the damning need to irrigate the thirst for blood found in a meat-based diet.

In this perfect place, the so-called "scholarly minds" don't exploit their animal brothers to test ego-driven hypotheses in torture chambers called laboratories. Indigenous people don't stretch animal hides over their backs and furniture to prove their status by mutilating those whose only fault is their inability to verbalize their suffering.

I've walked through continents whose only divisions are marked by the splendid diversity of landscape: mountains, rivers, plains, and plateaus; places where the only passport needed is genuine respect for all who live there.

On this Earth, the people are varied and unique. To see a

face of a different color is only one more reason to marvel at the rich imagination of the Creator. Furthermore, there is no iron-handed government hiding black secrets, believing its lies are clever enough that its evil will be overlooked.

This vision haunts me. I wonder about its purpose. Is it a concoction of my own imagination? An oasis for a mind struggling to survive in a world it finds thoroughly incomprehensible? Or is it some distant, parallel reality that has connected to me through roots of hope so deep they have reached some mirror universe? In a holographic paradigm an equal and opposite must exist as surely as there is night and day.

I want to believe it is something more! A prophetic picture of *our* future! A blueprint that has been etched into my heart, perhaps by an aspect of All That Is not restricted to linear perception; by a consciousness that can travel through time. Whether this fantasy was given to me by an alien or a portion of my own soul, which may be one and the same, it has more power over me than anything else.

With such an enormous goal of transforming an entire planet plagued by years of egocentric thinking, my prayers to be of assistance were answered: go get certified as a hypnotherapist! Not what I had anticipated, but then again, who am I to question the authority of a higher being? Someone once said to me, "If God told you to do something, you would be happy to do it no matter what it was."

This new job I've been assigned, helping abductees remove

memory blocks, may seem insignificant compared to the other challenges here on Earth, but who can comprehend the intricate tapestry of life? Perhaps people of contact have indeed "inherited knowledge of great importance" that can only be extracted at precisely the right timing. Given all the variables of a changing world, the determination of that timing may need to be realized instinctively, rather than by a designated date. When the mass consciousness is ready, perhaps a desire on behalf of abductees to further probe their minds for forgotten memories may elicit some jewels of information imparted to them at those large assemblies in the "complex," where we were "being prepared for something."

Even if contactees haven't been implanted with special wisdom, one of us via telepathy could have accidentally tripped across the psychic schematic of an alien energy source or technological wonder that could solve the energy and social problems of our world. Then again, maybe nothing special lives within the abductee other than an occasional new hybrid life-form.

If the reason I was urged to get certified—which, by the way, I did immediately—has no more hidden meaning than helping one or two people live more productive lives, I'm perfectly honored to help. I am still a commercial photographer. I do not desire to become a full-time hypnotherapist, but when people find me and they have a need, I will be there for them. At the same time, I follow my vision, but I suspect my two paths are intimately intertwined.

closure

CONCLUSION

Knowing what I know about the aliens' existence and all the information I've extracted from my abductions leaves me exiled from living a normal life. Sometimes I feel like a leper, and yet there are times I could not imagine my life another way. I know secrets men and women pray to know. I've been given experiential proof I am not limited to a physical body; proof other realms exist; proof we can and *are* evolving, even if it doesn't fit our pictures of how it should occur.

At times, the physical and psychological pain have defied description, but the terror forced me beyond my limitations. I discovered aspects and abilities of consciousness I could have found no other way, such as telepathy, clairvoyance, and tele-portation, though I have far from mastered them. Whether it is their intention or not, the aliens are "pressuring" us, in the truest sense of the word, to evolve.

Most importantly, what I've discovered through my journey is: evolution doesn't magically occur, evolution is a constant, sometimes brutal, struggle. The physical world and its inhabi-tants are pearls of evolution, and someone is desperately trying to salvage what they can of the millions of years of cultivation it took to get us here. Whether the aliens are here for their own reasons or are here intentionally aiding our development, their presence must be considered.

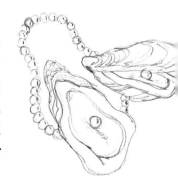

I can only think of four reasons individuals would want to

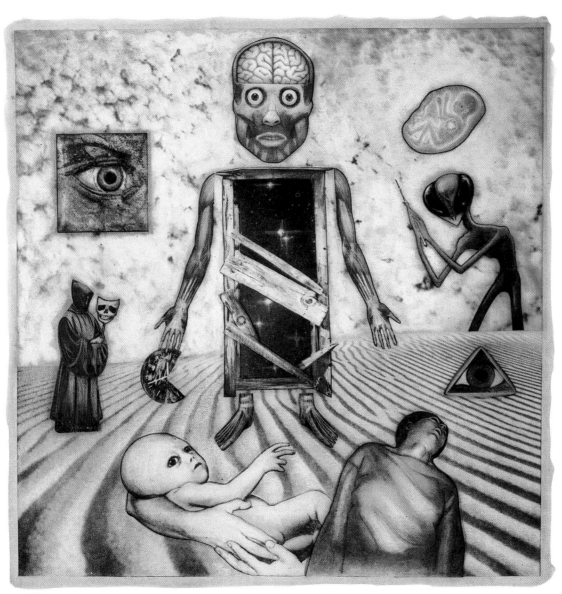

Mindscape

speak publicly about being abducted by aliens. Either they haven't got a life, they are acting stupidly, they are crazy, or they feel they have something important they need to communicate. In my own defense, I will address each possibility.

Before abduction I had an ideal life: a man I loved, a career I enjoyed, many dear friends and living was easy. To put it frankly, opening my mouth cost me the first; redirected the course of the second; and though my friends didn't abandon me, living in general is a thousand times more difficult.

Am I stupid for ever telling anyone? That's certainly possible, but I felt it was necessary to speak up, and I have no regrets.

Have I lost my sanity? Well, I passed the standard psychological tests. Of course, there are brilliant crazy people who can fool tests, but I don't think I fall into the category of brilliant or crazy. I'm just an average person who has had some not-so-average encounters.

Therefore, I would like to share something I consider to be important: I cannot prove aliens exist. I have no physical evidence acceptable to science. I only have my experiences and the effects they have had on me. Those effects have been soul-stirring.

The old saying, "You don't know what you have until you lose it," lives with me. It was sealed in my essence by the aliens. Knowing the grave concern they have for the way we are destroying ourselves suggests things are probably a lot worse than we have the foresight to imagine.

In fact, Earth's condition appears to be so critical that humans may someday be replaced with a new, improved species that is a whole lot smarter and doesn't have all of our emotional hang-ups. I hate to say it, but I think the Greys may have the right idea.

We humans are selfish, inconsiderate, and unconscious of our negative impact on Earth. If someone or something out there has the ability to correct the situation, and feels Earth has had enough of us, then more power to them. Whether we are going to be replaced by the hybrids, or whether the hybrid children are going to a world all their own, it is time for the destruction to stop.

There are millions of other species on this planet who don't have a say in the matter. They are at our mercy, and we are failing them.

Some people think it doesn't matter. Everything lives, everything dies, it's all part of life, right? So why bother to make any changes? Or the ultimate cop-out is: it's too late, anyway.

Well, those people are wrong. What we do here matters greatly, in more ways, in more directions, and in more dimensions than our limited brains can fathom, and until it is all over, it is never too late.

Like the "eyes" said, "If you know an unthinkable act is taking place and you turn your head, you are still guilty and responsible." We all know our planet's ecosystem is suffering,

and we know it can be changed by lending a helping hand or a helping heart. I doubt all of us will run out and become activists, although that would be wonderful, but I do believe, even with small gestures every day, we can collectively contribute to the healing of our Mother Earth and our fellow occupants upon this world. We don't need an alien race to beat us over the head before it's too late—or do we?

The Creator is here looking out for its creations, and the people of this planet could be in for a "rude awakening" of their own. The Creator may not be recognized as a man in a white robe. The Creator just might look like a giant insect with a needle in its hand saying it's time for us to get the point.

The point is, the Creator is not going to allow the entire Earthship to go down because one species has gone awry. We can be of assistance now, or be held responsible later…and we *will* be held responsible.

Whatever you consider God to be, my experiences have taught me that, in God's "eyes," this world is important and God is asking us to help. Love and respect yourselves and each other; love and respect all living things; and honor this unique portion of creation. It wasn't easy to come by and, if we *don't* wake up, no one else may have the opportunity to pass this way again. But if we *do* wake up, this world could be transformed into a magnificent vision of peace and harmony beyond our wildest dreams. ☻

Reflection

ABDUCTION QUESTIONNAIRE

If you suspect you or someone you know may be experiencing abduction phenomena, the following questionnaire is designed to assist in determining if further investigation may be warranted.

DREAMS

1. Do you dream of flying?

2. Do you dream of passing through windows, walls, or ceilings?

3. Do you dream of being underwater, and/or breathing underwater?

4. Do you dream of going unconscious?

5. Do you dream of choking on thick substances, like mud?

6. Do you dream about doctors or of being examined? (for women: gynecological, for men: genital or anal)

7. Do you dream of having sex with people you would not normally be attracted to? Dream of group sexual encounters

or have other unusual sexual dreams?

8. *(Women only)* Do you dream about pregnancy, giving birth, or breastfeeding?

9. Do you dream of seeing babies or children? If so, was there anything unusual about these babies or children?

10. Do you dream of eyes?

11. Do you dream of bugs or animals like deer, owls, wolves or grey cats?

12. Do you dream of being pursued or of rescuing or being rescued?

13. Do you dream of catastrophic events such as earthquakes, tidal waves, or nuclear war?

14. Do you dream you are in classrooms or taking unusual tests?

15. Do you dream about hospitals, underground facilities or large amphitheaters? Dream of interacting with military personnel?

16. Do you dream of barren, desertlike landscapes with adobe-style structures?

17. Do you dream of UFOs or alien beings?

PSYCHOLOGICAL ISSUES

1. Do you consider yourself to be more open-minded than the average person?

2. Do you believe in other realities and or experiment with altered states of consciousness?

3. Do you consider plants and animals as important as human beings?

4. Do you consider yourself to be an environmentalist?

5. Do you believe life exists on other planets?

6. Do you have any phobias, such as public speaking or claustrophobia?

7. Do you dislike doctors or dentists?

8. Do you have a phobia of needles?

9. Do you have insomnia or abnormal sleep patterns?

10. Do you sleep with a light, radio, or TV on, or must your bed be up against a wall?

11. Have you ever been afraid of your closet, now or as a child, or must the closet door be tightly closed before you go to sleep?

12. Do you awaken from sleep startled?

13. Do you often feel you are being watched?

14. Do you feel a compulsion to go to remote places for no reason?

15. Are there places you will avoid, such as stretches of road or underground parking structures?

16. Do you change your place of residence often?

17. Do you have memory gaps in your life, especially around childhood or puberty?

18. Have you ever felt you were "different" than others?

19. Are you adamant about not having children?

20. Are you extremely sexual?

21. Do you ever feel you are being watched while having sex?

22. Do you experience problems or discomfort with sex or relationships?

23. Do you watch the sky and stars with undue fascination, foreboding, or both?

24. Do you feel you may know something that you shouldn't talk about?

25. Have you ever felt an unseen presence nearby?

26. Do you have flashes or visions of alien faces?

ANOMALOUS PHENOMENA

1. Have you ever experienced extra or missing time, such as arriving much sooner or much later than you should have while driving somewhere?

2. Have you had, or do you have, out-of-body experiences?

3. Are you unusually psychic or telepathic?

4. Have you ever woken up without remembering having gone to sleep?

5. Have you ever woken up someplace other than where you remember going to sleep?

6. Have you ever woken up and found possessions or articles of clothing other than how you remember seeing them before you went to sleep?

7. Do your animals ever appear to be drugged or dazed for no apparent reason?

8. Does electrical and/or electronic equipment malfunction around you often, or do you find watches do not work on you for long?

9. Are you a vegetarian, or mostly so?

PHYSICAL PHENOMENA

1. Have you ever seen beams of light or balls of light that could not be explained?

2. Have you ever heard unusual rushing, buzzing, or high-pitched sounds?

3. Have you ever experienced strange, pungent odors—like burning wire or rotting organic material—without being able to locate the source?

4. Has your car suddenly stalled and later restarted for no reason, or has your radio or television filled with static even when turned off?

5. Have you ever seen unusual mists or fogs where none should have been?

6. Have you ever seen strangely shaped, isolated clouds that did not move with the other clouds?

7. Have you ever seen a UFO, or stars in the sky making unusual or impossible maneuvers?

8. Have you ever seen unusual beings?

9. Have you ever seen black, unmarked helicopters or cars, or seen strange-looking men dressed in black suits around your neighborhood?

YOUR PHYSICAL BODY

1. Do you wake up after an adequate amount of sleep still feeling tired or drugged?

2. Do you ever wake up during the night feeling paralyzed or unable to move your body right away?

3. Do you ever have headaches, especially behind one eye?

4. Did you ever wake up with nosebleeds, or have nosebleeds for no apparent reason?

5. Do you have sinus problems?

6. Do you have extremely good hearing?

7. Are you sensitive to certain sounds or lights?

8. Do you ever have earaches, or ringing in your ears?

9. Do you have low vital signs (i.e., blood pressure, body temperature, heart rate)?

10. Do you ever have a hard time breathing?

11. Are you sensitive to medications?

12. Are you sensitive to consumer products such as soaps or perfumes?

13. Do you ever wake up with bruises, scratches, cuts, soreness, or scars that cannot be explained?

14. Do you ever wake up with sore genitals that cannot be explained?

(*For Women Only*)

15. Do you have female problems such as painful periods?

16. Have you ever missed periods and didn't know why?

17. Have you ever thought you were pregnant, whether confirmed or not, and later found out you were not?

18. Have you ever had an unusual miscarriage?

(*For Men Only*)

19. Do you have a lump or lumps on your testicles?

WHERE TO FIND HELP

If you answered yes to a majority of the questions and/or you suspect you are experiencing "abduction phenomena" and would like further help or information, assistance is available in many cities through the Mutual UFO Network (MUFON), or through the Center for UFO Studies (CUFOS).

The Mutual UFO Network (MUFON)
103 Oldtowne Road
Seguin, TX 78155-4099

The Center for UFO Studies (CUFOS)
2437 West Peterson Avenue
Chicago, IL 60659

HOW TO STOP ABDUCTION

The abduction questionnaire was designed to determine if contact may be happening to you or someone you know. If you believe you may be experiencing contact, the following suggestions may be of assistance.

I wish I had the magic pill and could say take two of these and call me in the morning, but unfortunately I cannot do that—yet! What I *can* give are some methods which I have developed on my own that seem to be working consistently. I realize there are many forms of contact occurring on this planet at this time and I do not assume all of them to be of a negative nature. I do know, for reasons I've already mentioned, that most contact remains hidden from our normal consciousness.

The first step, then, is to become fully cognitive of the interactions as they are occurring. After this level is achieved, you can then decide if the contacts are beneficial.

Now that I am a hypnotherapist, I realize the formula I developed years ago, on my own, was nothing more than self-hypnosis. My belief that the subconscious is all-knowing was the key to my success. I programmed my subconscious to come to my rescue by reciting the following affirmations every night as I fell asleep:

I deserve to be conscious of my total self and all of my experience.

I am always aware and in control of all aspects of myself.

I can and will maintain full awareness throughout each contact.

I deserve to be conscious.

I deserve to be conscious.

I deserve to be conscious.

After months of repeating this affirmation, my subconscious developed techniques to wake me into full consciousness just before or during an abduction. I was pleasantly surprised at the creative solutions this "other part" of me contrived. I believe that if this process is applied with absolute intention for success, you, too, will find a new source of creative potential just waiting to be utilized.

The emphasis here is intention. Merely reciting words without full expectation of having them realized is useless. If the fear of facing the unknown is stronger than the desire to know the truth, the fear must be dealt with first. This can be accomplished in any manner that feels appropriate. I have found one of the best ways to deal with fear is by accumulating as much knowledge as possible about that which is feared. There have been many valuable books published in recent years on the subject of abduction which I have included in "Suggested Reading." Therapy also can help desensitize the fear, though it is still difficult to find qualified therapists who are familiar with the abduction phenomena.

If you have had success with the first part of this formula—have had partial or full conscious experiences—you are probably

feeling more confident and powerful than before. If you have come to the conclusion that abduction is not something you prefer, you have already developed a working relationship with your subconscious and can further employ it to stop the abductions altogether.

Most abductions occur at night. The aliens wait until we are already asleep so it is easier to manipulate the brain. The trick is to train the sleeping mind to recognize when this control is being applied. Once the subconscious has learned to recognize the intrusion and has learned to alert you, the rest is up to the conscious self.

Most likely you will find yourself in a semi-conscious state, feeling drugged and/or paralyzed or partially so. This is the hardest part. It takes a lot of power, physically and mentally, to fight off the paralysis and psychic domination. You must keep telling yourself, "I will wake up completely, I will win." What works for me when I feel completely paralyzed is to concentrate on one part of my body: my head, hands, or feet. Once I manage to move my head from side to side I can break free completely.

You will feel like giving up and going back to sleep...don't. That's exactly what they want! The aliens are reluctant to abduct us if we are awake and in charge of our bodies; they are afraid of our anger and our physical strength.

I believe all sentient beings in creation are telepathically connected at some level, so I suspected a part of me would always know when the Greys were thinking about abducting

me. When I decided I wanted the abductions to stop, I started reciting the following affirmations:

My subconscious loves me and wants to protect me.

My subconsciousness will always know when the aliens are thinking about me and will wake me up.

I will always know when they are coming and I will always be able to stop them.

Of course, if you have a particular faith, backing up the affirmations with mention of the deity of your spiritual belief can only give them more power:

With the help of God, I can and will stop abduction every time.

I deserve to be left alone. I deserve to be free.

I have been told that affirmations should always be worded in a positive statement. "With the help of God, I can stop abduction," could be rephrased, "With God's love, my nights are safe and secure." But I believe it is the energy and idea behind the words that carries the power. Write your own affirmations or use the ones I've suggested but most of all know you have the power, because you do.

I have had great success at stopping abductions, but I've discovered, in my case, the aliens never give up. They still continue to try and abduct me. Unfortunately fighting abduction is like fighting alcoholism: it's one day at a time…every day.

After so many years of training my subconscious, I don't need the affirmations on a regular basis anymore; they have

become a part of my belief system. Be patient and believe in yourself. I wish for you all the restful nights you desire and deserve. ☻

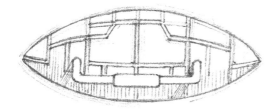

SUGGESTED READING

Friedman, Stanton. *Crash at Corona*. New York: Paragon Press, 1992.

Hopkins, Budd. *Missing Time*. New York: Ballantine Books, 1988.

_____. *Intruders*. New York: Random House, 1987.

Howe, Linda Moulton. *Glimpses of Other Realities*. Huntingdon Valley, PA: LMH Productions, 1993.

Jacobs, David. *Secret Life*. New York: Simon & Schuster, 1992.

Mack, John. *Abduction: Human Encounters with Aliens*. New York: Macmillan Publishing, 1994.

Rifkin, Jeremy. *Beyond Beef*. New York: Penguin Books, 1993.

Ring, Kenneth, Ph.D. *The Omega Project*. New York: William Morrow & Co., 1992.

Robbins, John. *Diet for a New America*. Hanover, NH: Stillpoint Publishing, 1987.

Royal, Lyssa, and Keith Priest. *Visitors From Within*. Phoenix, AZ: Royal Priest Research Press, 1992.

Strieber, Whitley. *Communion*. New York: Avon Books, 1987.

_____. *Transformation*. New York: Avon Books, 1988.

ABOUT THE AUTHOR

Kim Carlsberg was born and raised in Kansas City, Missouri. At the age of twenty, she moved to Los Angeles, California, where she has resided for nineteen years.

A graduate of Los Angeles Art Center College of Design in commercial photography, Kim is also a member of IATSE, local 659, the motion picture and television camera operators' union.

Kim's career as a fine art and professional celebrity photographer has covered all aspects of the entertainment and music industries, and has included photographing the president of the United States.

As a vegetarian, an animal rights activist, and an impassioned environmentalist, her primary life goals are spiritual and humanitarian.

ABOUT THE ARTIST

Darryl Anka was born in Ottawa, Canada, and has lived in Los Angeles for most of his life. He began his career in graphic design, which eventually led to designing special effects for such projects as *Star Trek, Babylon 5,* and many other film and television productions.

Darryl is also an internationally acclaimed channel who has conducted interactive workshops and motivational seminars for over a decade.

He has been active in UFO research since he experienced two close-proximity daylight sightings in Los Angeles in 1973.

Correspondence to the author and illustrator should be mailed to:

Kim Carlsberg/Darryl Anka
P.O. Box 8307
Calabasas, CA 91302

HAVE YOU HAD AN EXTRATERRESTRIAL ENCOUNTER?

The authors are looking for illustrations and paintings (full color whenever possible) from you for a new and unique publication. We would like one representation of your most interesting experience. Illustrations may be amateur or professional. If you know an artist who can render your experience, it is perfectly acceptable to have them do so.

You may use any medium or style you feel best exhibits the qualities of your encounter. Please render drawings or paintings into a square format no larger that ten inches by ten inches, and no smaller than six inches by six inches. Include a written description of the experience.

The purpose of this publication is to further demonstrate the reality, frequency and wide range of close encounters around the world. All reproduction of the artwork received will be handled with the highest integrity and professionalism. Due to the large numbers of submissions we anticipate, we may not be able to return the art. If time permits, we will make every effort to do so. Reproduction-quality transparencies of the art are acceptable.

Unless you wish to remain anonymous, you will receive full written credit in the publication for your entry, so be sure to include your full name and address on the back of your artwork submission and please print clearly.

We are excited about your participation in this ground-breaking work. If your submission is accepted for publication, you will receive a notice by mail as to the name and date of the publication.

Send to: Encounter Art
P.O. Box 8307
Calabasas, CA 91302

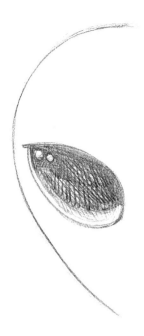

Beyond My Wildest Dreams

BOOKS OF RELATED INTEREST
BY BEAR & COMPANY

BRINGERS OF THE DAWN
Teachings from the Pleiadians
by Barbara Marciniak

DOLPHINS, ETs & ANGELS
Adventures Amoung Spiritual Intelligences
by Timothy Wyllie

EARTH
Pleiadian Keys to the Living Library
by Barbara Marciniak

HEART OF THE CHRISTOS
Starseeding from the Pleiades
by Barbara Hand Clow

THE MAYAN ORACLE
Return Path to the Stars
by Ariel Spilsbury and Michael Bryner

SIGNET OF ATLANTIS
War in Heaven Bypass
by Barbara Hand Clow

THE 12TH PLANET
by Zecharia Sitchin

Contact your local bookseller

~ or ~

BEAR & COMPANY
P.O. Box 2860
Santa Fe, NM 87504
1-800-WE-BEARS